Where Will You Be When You Get Where You're Going?

Where Will You Be When You Get Where You're Going?

Leonard E. Stadler

Bristol House

**WHERE WILL YOU BE WHEN YOU
GET WHERE YOU'RE GOING?**
© 2000 by Leonard E. Stadler
Published by Bristol Books, an imprint of Bristol House, Ltd.

First Edition, December 2000
Second Printing, February 2003
Third Printing, July 2004

Unless otherwise indicated, all Scripture quotations are from
the *New King James Version* © 1979, 1980, 1982 by Thomas
Nelson Publishers, Nashville, Tennessee.

ISBN: 1-885224-31-1

Printed in the United States of America

Cover design by Larry Stuart.

Bristol House, Ltd.
1201 E. 5th Street, Suite 2107
Anderson, Indiana 46012
Phone: 765-644-0856
Fax: 765-622-1045

To order call: 1-800-451-READ (7323)

In Memory of Dr. Paul L. Morell
Father-in-Law, Mentor and Friend

Trust in the Lord with all your heart,
And lean not on your own understanding;
In all your ways acknowledge Him,
and He shall direct your paths
(Proverbs 3:5-6).

Contents

··

Foreword

The great days of the church have been days of great preaching. We have gone through a period when the emphasis has been on the liturgy to the neglect of preaching. This is one reason that we have seen the decline of mainline churches. I have discovered when there is fire in the pulpit there will be people in the pews. Because of the excellent quality of preaching, Dr. Stadler's church (Weddington United Methodist Church, Weddington, North Carolina) is one of the fastest growing congregations in North Carolina.

These messages are evangelical sermons at their best. There are superb illustrations, rich content and appropriate subjects. They are biblical yet contemporary and relevant.

I heard Bishop William C. Martin once say he had never had a church to ask for a counselor or an administrator. He said they all asked for a pastor who can preach.

I recommend this book to pastors and laypersons. They will be inspired and strengthened by these unique messages.

There is an evangelical awakening taking place around the world. God is raising up a new generation of preachers to lead the way. Dr. Lenny Stadler will be one of them.

—Dr. Edmund W. Robb

Introduction

Enter by the narrow gate; for wide is the gate and broad is the way that leads to destruction, and there are many who go in by it. Because narrow is the gate and difficult is the way which leads to life, and there are few who find it (Matthew 7:13-14).

I heard about a man who boarded a bus with the full intention of going to Detroit. At the end of the long trip when he got off the bus, he found himself not in Detroit but in Kansas City, Missouri. Somehow, he had boarded the wrong bus!

Unfortunately, something like that happens too often in human life. People intend to go one place but they end up somewhere else. Most of us want the "good life." We want happiness and security. We want long-lasting and meaningful relationships. We want productive careers and useful lives. Our intentions may be good, but sometimes we catch the wrong bus and end up in the wrong place.

Back in the 1970s I traveled in a contemporary Christian music group. We performed and recorded Christian songs. We wrote one song entitled "Where Will You Be When You Get Where You're Going?" There is a message in that song title, and it is still appropriate for us today.

The man who started to Detroit and ended in Kansas City could not believe what happened. He caught a cab and told the driver to take him to Woodward Avenue. When the driver told him there was no Woodward Avenue in the city, he became indignant: "Now see here, I know Detroit and I have been on Woodward Avenue many times in this city. Don't tell me that there is no Woodward Avenue in this city." The cabbie replied, "Sir, this is not Detroit. This is Kansas City!" Then it dawned on the man that despite the clarity of his desire and the sincerity of his intentions, he had caught the wrong bus and ended up in the wrong place.

This is a great parable for us today. It can happen so easily to us. The Prodigal Son did not start out intending to end up in the pigpen. It was not his planned destination. He went to the "far country" in search of happiness and excitement, fulfillment and freedom, but he caught the wrong bus and ended up in the wrong place!

I have performed many wedding ceremonies for young, happy couples. When I meet with these couples, most are infatuated with each other. They have a sparkle in their eyes, an excitement in their voices, and a love in their hearts for each other. They intend to have happy homes and healthy marriages. Since I witness so many marriages ending in divorce, I find myself praying under my breath, "Oh Lord, help them to get on the right bus!" Husbands and wives, where will your marriage be when you get where you're going? Are you on the right bus?

I see parents who want only the best for their children. They work tirelessly to provide for their college tuition. They hope they will end up with high morals and values. They deeply desire for their children to have a personal relationship with Jesus Christ. They assume that their children will grow into a strong faith. But good intentions are not enough. Parents, where will your children be when you get where you're going?

The same thing can happen to each one of us. Many of us have high ideals and worthy goals. We want meaning and fulfillment. We want happiness and acceptance. We want spiritual wisdom, a steady prayer life, a good command of the Scriptures, a close walk with God, and respect from others. But the critical question arises, where will **YOU** be when you get where you're going?

In our everyday conversation, we have certain phrases we use to underscore the problem. We say things such as, "He is headed for a fall," "She is on a collision course," "That marriage is getting off track," and "Those young people are way out in left field."

What about you and me? Are we on the road that is leading us to the right place? Are we doing the things that will assure us of our intended destination? If you stay on your present course, where will it lead? If you get where you are going, where will you be?

We all want salvation. We all want eternal life. We all want the abundant life that Jesus came to give us. But the question still comes to us: Are we willing to make the necessary commitment? Are we willing to go down the narrow road? Are we willing to walk through the narrow gate? The narrow gate or the broad, easy way—which will it be for you and me?

What is this narrow gate? It is the way of commitment! It is the way of dedication, sacrifice, single-mindedness, determination, discipline, purpose and devotion.

Everyone wants to be somebody but few want to pay the price. Many people want gain without pain, triumph without trying, something for nothing, victory without sacrifice. But life does not work that way. The gate is narrow. The way to abundant life is the way of total commitment.

One of the reasons I enjoy the *Peanuts* comic strip is because of Charlie Brown. In many ways Charlie Brown represents our innermost feelings. He highlights human nature in a dramatic and honest way.

On one occasion Charlie comes to Lucy Van Pelt for five-cents worth of psychological advice. Charlie says to Lucy, "Dr. Lucy, I need help. I just don't feel a sense of commitment to anything. I don't seem to be able to find a direction or purpose for my life." Psychologist Lucy responds, "Well, Charlie Brown, life is like an ocean liner making its way through the sea. Some folks put their deck chairs facing the front of the ship. Some folks put their deck chairs facing the side of the ship. And other folks place their deck chairs facing the back of the ship. The question is, Charlie Brown, which direction are you facing?" Charlie answers sadly, "I can't even unfold the deck chair!"

All of us feel like that at times. But then God brings someone across our path who has gone through the narrow gate of commitment to inspire us. Take the world of sports. On February 20, 1988, in Calgary, Alberta, Brian Boitano won the Olympic gold medal for the United States. He went on to become one of the greatest figure skaters of all time. When you watch him skate, it is easy to think that he is a natural. But that is far from the truth. There is no such thing as a natural-born skater. Brian Boitano has been skating five hours a day, six days a week, for the last twenty-three years! That is why he is an Olympic champion, a world-class skater. He has passed through the narrow gate of commitment to ice skating.

It's true in sports, academics, music—and it's true in the Christian life. What would happen in your life or mine if we spent five hours a day, six days a week, for twenty-three years praying and studying the Bible?

This makes me think about the life of John Bunyan. They arrested John Bunyan because he was preaching Christ. He stayed in prison for twelve years because of his faith. At the end of the twelfth year, the authorities came to him and said, "John Bunyan, we are going to set you free on one condition—that you promise not to preach about Christ anymore." John Bunyan replied, "I am determined yet to suffer until moss grows over my eyebrows rather than to violate my faith in Christ Jesus, my Lord."

There is a great temptation to choose the path of least resistance. We tend to settle for a sentimental, soothing, spoon-fed kind of religion that will require nothing of us. The great symbol of the Christian faith is not a pew cushion or an easy chair. It is an old rugged cross! If we are going to walk with Jesus, we have to pass through the narrow gate of commitment to Christ.

Are you committed? I mean, are you really committed to Christ and to His Church with your heart, soul, mind and strength? The gospel is free but its cost is met by those who are convinced that Jesus Christ is the way, the truth and the life.

A certain teenage boy always seemed to be in trouble, having a hard time growing up. He was disruptive, disagreeable and disgruntled with life. As a result of his involvement in many fights he had earned the name, "Bruiser." In fact everyone called him, "Bruiser Johnson." Most people thought Bruiser was a hopeless case. He was certainly on the wrong bus. Many thought his destination would eventually lead him to reform school or to prison.

However, a caring youth counselor in the church became interested in Bruiser, reaching out to him and befriending him. He listened to and encouraged the youth. He helped him at every opportunity. Over time, Bruiser Johnson was so touched by the Christian commitment of the youth counselor that he recognized the Spirit of Christ in him. Bruiser accepted Jesus Christ as his Lord and Savior, stopped fighting and started living for Christ. He was still rough on the edges, but he was now tenderhearted and kind to others. He soon joined the church and got active in the youth program.

On one occasion the pastor invited him to pray in the morning worship service. The worship bulletin read, "Prelude . . . Johann Sebastian Bach" and "Prayer of Invocation . . . Bruiser Johnson." That morning, Bruiser stepped into the pulpit and prayed: "Oh God, bless all the people here who are old. And, oh God, bless all the people here who are young. And, oh God, bless all the rest who are in the middle. And help us all to love each other and be committed to you, for Christ's sake." When Bruiser Johnson said "amen" and sat down, not a dry eye was in the house. He never became a famous person. He was just an ordinary person who had been touched by God's love and responded by dedicating his life to Christ.

Some years later, that church ran a survey of its members and asked a series of questions about the church. One of the questions in the survey was this: "When did you experience the presence of God in our church most powerfully?" The response was amazing. A large number of people answered, "The day Bruiser Johnson prayed in church!"

The practical sermons that follow here are written to be heard. My prayer is that they will increase awareness, inspire reflection, and provoke discussion on the Christian life in the world today. One hopes that these messages will be found relevant and applicable.

As you read, you will have many opportunities to choose the road you will take and the way by which you will get to where you want to go. Ask yourself, "Which road am I traveling? Am I on the right bus? Since God wants only the best for me, am I on schedule with Him? Is my present course leading me into a deeper personal relationship with Jesus Christ? Or is it taking me further down the broad, easy way that leads to nowhere?" Still, the overall question is: "Where will you be when you get where you're going?"

Chapter 1

Key Ingredients of an Effective Faith

Now after John was put in prison, Jesus came to Galilee, preaching the gospel of the kingdom of God, and saying, "The time is fulfilled, and the kingdom of God is at hand. Repent, and believe in the gospel."

And as He walked by the Sea of Galilee, He saw Simon and Andrew his brother casting a net into the sea; for they were fishermen. Then Jesus said to them, "Follow Me, and I will make you become fishers of men." They immediately left their nets and followed Him.

When He had gone a little farther from there, He saw James the son of Zebedee, and John his brother, who also were in the boat mending their nets. And immediately He called them, and they left their father Zebedee in the boat with the hired servants, and went after Him (Mark 1:14-20).

. . . .

The matter of faith is always at the forefront of the Christian life. We hear people say, "Have faith! Keep the faith! Receive the faith! Learn the faith! Share the faith! Proclaim the faith! Live the faith!" But what does this really mean?

More often than not, we seek a "user-friendly" kind of faith. We want to hear about a faith that will reassure us, not one that will challenge us. We want a faith that will soothe us; not one that will aggravate us.

In our world, Christians need to be on the cutting edge of faith. Consider these key ingredients of a vital Christian faith. When they are blended into our daily lives, the result will be a faith that is active, alive and effective.

My grandmother had the fine reputation of being one of the best cooks in the county. She was known especially for her brown sugar pies and cakes. Now, any good cook can bake pies and cakes, but my grandmother had key ingredients that made hers superior. When she blended them into the regular recipe, the result was a delicious dessert.

In the 1930s, a man who had been walking across the desert for several days was dying of thirst. But he stumbled upon an old water pump. A baking soda can hung from the pump handle. Inside the can there was a note signed "Desert Pete." The note read: "This pump is all right as of June, 1932. I put a new washer in and it should last five years. But the washer dries out and the pump has to be primed. Under the white rock, I buried a bottle of water. It's out of the sun and corked up. There is enough water in the bottle to prime the pump, but not if you drink some first. Pour about one-fourth of the water into the pump, and let it soak the leather. Then pour the rest of the water around the joints and pump like crazy. You'll get water! After you drink, fill the bottle up again and put it back like you found it for the next person." Then there was this P.S. "Remember: Don't drink the water in the bottle. Prime the pump with it, and you'll get water. Just have faith!"

In his homespun way, Desert Pete has graphically described the basic ingredients of the Christian faith. What are the key ingredients of faith? *Trust! Risk! Serve!* We trust in Jesus Christ and His work of redemption for the salvation of our souls. We risk our lives for His cause and kingdom! We serve to win and disciple others in the name and Spirit of Christ.

These ingredients are dramatically present in Mark 1. Jesus said, "Follow Me! I will make you fishers of men and women. Come and join me. We will fish for the hearts and souls of people." Look how those fishermen responded: They immediately threw down their nets, left their boats and followed Him. Talk about trust, risk and serve! They dropped everything and followed Him.

The word "follow" means "obedience." It is the kind of obedience a soldier gives to a commanding officer. It means "commitment." It is the kind of commitment that is unflinching, unswerving, unwavering and unshakable. It means "love." It is the kind of love that is total and sacrificial. It means "devotion." It is the kind of devotion that calls us to lay our lives on the line for a cause greater than ourselves.

Jesus is calling us to follow Him in a life of faith and Christian discipleship. He is asking for our obedience, commitment, love and devotion. Jesus is asking for our hearts, souls, minds and strength. He is asking for us to trust in Him, to risk for Him and to work with Him. These are the key ingredients in the Christian faith.

Trust

TRUST is the first key ingredient. In Christian theology, it is called "the leap of faith." It is trusting in God to be with us throughout all of life, no matter what happens.

About one hundred years ago, an elderly man was traveling alone on a train in France. A much younger man was sitting next to him. He watched as the older man pulled out a Bible and began reading it. After awhile the younger man decided to strike up a conversation with the older gentleman and asked, "What are you reading?"

The older man smiled and replied, "I'm reading from the sixth chapter of John's Gospel in the New Testament."

"What does it say?" asked the younger man.

"Well, it's about the feeding of the five thousand. It is the miracle of the loaves and fishes."

Scornfully and cynically, the younger man said, "You don't really believe that stuff, do you?"

The older man replied, "Well, of course, I do!" To which the younger man said, "I can see that you have been brainwashed by ancient superstition, but not me. You see, I am a scientist. The only thing I can trust and believe in is what can be proved scientifically. The story you have read defies the laws of science. Therefore, I could never accept that. As a man of science, I have no faith in miracles. Of course, I really don't expect you to understand that."

At this point, the train began to slow down. "Here's my station," said the young man. "It was nice talking with you. By the way, I didn't get your name."

The older man reached into his coat pocket, pulled out his business card, and handed it to the young man. The young man could not believe the name as he read it aloud: "Dr. Louis Pasteur!" Of course, Pasteur was one of the great scientists of all time. He was also a man of great faith. He knew that the scientific method, valuable as it is, was not the only road to truth.

The real truth is that the best things in life cannot be proven in a science laboratory: love, courage, integrity, honesty and faith. Faith is the capacity to trust beyond what we can see and touch and feel. Faith enables us to trust God's Messenger, Jesus Christ, and His message of salvation. Trust is an essential ingredient in faith.

Risk

RISK is the second key ingredient. Sooner or later, we have to stop playing it safe and follow God into the unknown. A Middle East chieftain tells about a spy who was captured and sentenced to death in the Persian army. The Persian general had a strange custom. He would give condemned criminals a choice between the firing squad and the big black door in his office. As the moment for execution drew near, a particular spy was brought before the Persian general. "What will it be? The firing squad, or the big black door?" The condemned spy hesitated for a long time. It was a difficult decision. Eventually, he chose the firing squad. Moments later, shots rang out confirming the execution. The Persian general turned to his lieutenant and said, "Isn't that something? They always prefer the known way to the unknown way." The lieutenant asked, "Well, what lies beyond the big black door?" The general replied, "Freedom! Only a very few have been brave enough to risk and go into the unknown."

This story reminds us how difficult it is to take a risk. It is not easy to take the leap of faith. The temptation is to stay with the familiar, and not to venture into the unknown. Often, we want to take only a calculated risk. We are not too keen on risking life or limb. An old proverb states, "He who risks too little gains too little."

Jesus came to the seashore and called to Simon, Andrew, James, and John to follow Him. Look what happened! They turned from their boats and dropped their familiar nets. They followed Him out into an unknown future, where together they turned the world upside down.

Are you ready to take a risky leap of faith? Will you step out and follow Christ? Will you give your life to Him as never before—with all your heart, mind, soul and strength? If you will take the risk, if you will make the leap of faith, God will bless you, and incredible things will happen in your life.

Serve

SERVING is the third key ingredient. Simon, Andrew, James and John did not work their way to discipleship. The gift of faith was freely given. But as soon as they became disciples, Jesus gave them a job. "Follow me, and I will make you fishers of men." A call to discipleship is a call to serve. It is a call to action and a call to work.

Have you heard the story about four angels who witnessed creation? The first angel observed God's handiwork in awe and said, "Lord, your creation is beautiful! How did you do it?" This is the worldview of a scientist.

The second angel observed in awe and said, "Lord, your creation is beautiful! Why did you do it?" This is the worldview of a philosopher.

The third angel observed in awe and said, "Lord, your creation is beautiful! How can I have it?" This is the worldview of a materialist.

The fourth angel observed in awe and said, "Lord, your creation is beautiful! Where can I work in it?" This is the worldview of a servant.

After we have accepted Jesus Christ as Savior and Lord, we should come to the church asking, "Lord, how can I help? What do you want me to do? Where can I serve? How can I be used for Your cause?"

Throughout the Bible, we see this over and over. People sense the presence of God. They have a divine encounter with Him. Then God puts them to work, and they are given a task.

We see it throughout the Scriptures: Moses encountered God in a burning bush, and God sent him to set His people free. Isaiah saw the Lord high and lifted up in the temple. It was a time of turmoil in the land. God needed a prophet for the hour. Isaiah responded, "Here am I, Lord, send me."

Peter, Andrew, James and John saw Jesus walking along the shore of the Sea of Galilee. They sensed His majesty and fell before Him. Jesus told them to get up and to follow Him into a life of discipleship.

Homer and Emmylou were courting on the front-porch swing. Homer was much in love with Emmylou, but he was shy. He had difficulty expressing his love. He tried a flowery approach. "Emmylou, if I had a thousand eyes, they would all be looking at you. Emmylou, if I had a thousand arms, they would all be hugging you. Emmylou, if I had a thousand lips, they would all be kissing you." To which Emmylou said, "Homer, why don't you just stop complaining about what you don't have and use what you do have?"

The point is clear: Talking a good game is not enough. Going through the rituals, reciting the creeds, singing the hymns, preaching the sermons or teaching the Sunday school lessons are not enough. Only when our creeds become deeds does our faith spring to life.

Trust! Risk! Serve! We *trust* in Jesus Christ and His work of redemption for the salvation of our souls. We *risk* our lives for His cause and kingdom. We *serve* to win and disciple others in the name and Spirit of Christ.

Where will you be when you get where you're going— with the key ingredients of an effective Christian faith?

Chapter 2

America: A Divine Calling

If My people who are called by My name will humble themselves, and pray and seek My face, and turn from their wicked ways, then I will hear from heaven, and will forgive their sin and heal their land (2 Chronicles 7:14).

. . . .

Where will America be when it gets where it's going? Does God have a plan for America? Is there a divine call upon this nation?

I grew up in the 1960s during the Woodstock generation. It was a turbulent and rebellious time in American history. The revolt was aimed against authority and morality. Growing long hair, protesting against the Vietnam conflict and advocating free love were all part of the rebellion.

However, when Jesus Christ came into my life, my eyes were open to many truths. One truth to which I had been blinded was the true greatness of this nation, and the conviction that God has a plan for America.

When you personally discover the reality of the living Christ, you also discover that God has a plan for your life as well, which can be discerned and followed through obedience and faith. If God deals with each of us on an individual basis, and if God has a plan for each of us, then may we not logically conclude that God deals with nations in the same way?

The Bible says that the Jews were God's chosen people, and that if they would obey His commandments, He would bless them as a nation. Deuteronomy is explicit about the covenant relationship between God and Israel.

Throughout their history, as long as the Israelites kept their end of the covenant, God blessed them. Yet as God began to do so, the Israelites inevitably turned away from Him, often in less than a generation. The people became so complacent and hard of heart that they stoned the prophets whom God sent to warn them to turn from their wicked ways and to seek God's forgiveness. When they repented, God restored their nation. This cycle of obedience—disobedience—judgment—repentance—restoration was repeated over and over in the history of Israel. The same is true for America today.

Peter Marshall, Jr., son of the late Senate chaplain, states that "America was a divine experiment." Nearly four hundred years ago our forefathers came to this land in response to God's call. The people who founded America had a common commitment to God. From its inception, this nation was based upon the principles of God's Word.

As early as 1620, this land became the great frontier of Western Christendom. It was to be a land of religious freedom where God could be worshiped in spirit and in truth, without hindrance by Britain. These people were brought together to fulfill a special calling.

The settlers who first came here sensed strongly the leadership of the Spirit of Jesus Christ. An opening phrase in the Mayflower Compact reads, "Having undertaken for the

Glory of God, and Advancement of the Christian Faith. . . ." The pilgrims were convinced that Jesus Christ had called them to North America to found a place of religious freedom for Puritans. The Mayflower Compact also declared that they would form a civil government.

You might be thinking, "Well, what is so unique about that?" It is unique because it is the only time in human history that a free group of men and women had the opportunity to form their own civil government based on the Word of God.

These were not nominal churchgoers. They were not seeking only religious freedom. Their lives had been radically changed by Jesus Christ. God had given them a vision for a new society. They believed that it was possible to establish the kingdom of God on earth.

This did not mean that everyone had to be a Christian. It did not mean that everyone would be required to go to church, or to force Christianity upon all the people. It did mean that enough of them had to be totally committed to Christ so that God's Word would be the foundation of our society.

I am convinced that God has given us a sacred trust of self-government under Him! That's why Abraham Lincoln said, "America is the last best hope on earth."

In 1776, when the fifty-six delegates to the Continental Congress signed the Declaration of Independence, a hush fell over the room. The late afternoon sun fired a brass candlestick on the tablecloth. The men gazed out the window, some with tears in their eyes, and some prayed. Their chairman, John Hancock, broke the silence: "Gentlemen, the price on my head has just doubled!" A chuckle followed. Samuel Adams stood to his feet and had the last word on that day: "We have this day restored this land to the Sovereign, to whom alone men ought to be obedient. He reigns in heaven and . . . from the rising to the setting sun, may His Kingdom come!"

Despite the claims of some historians, George Washington, the first president of our country, was not a deist. He was a deeply committed Christian. A deist is a person who believes in a transcendent, impersonal God. That is, God is so far removed from this world that He cannot be personally known.

Washington's mother was a devout Christian woman, and she had a great influence on her son. On one occasion, she said to him, "George, do not neglect the duty of secret prayer." Washington heeded her request, and he never neglected the duty of prayer. In fact, he spent a great deal of his adult life on his knees.

One answer to prayer for George Washington came on August 28, 1776. He and the Continental Army were on the beaches below Brooklyn Heights, New York. They were in a tight situation. The British troops had surrounded them. The only way of escape was to cross the East River to Manhattan Island. The general and his troops quietly assembled on the shore. Here, they boarded every small boat available, and they ferried across the river to Manhattan. However, the evacuation was taking too long. At any moment the British would see what was happening. General Washington prayed and an amazing thing happened, the most astonishing weather event that occurred in the war. A dense fog suddenly covered the area. Both the British and American troops were hidden under the canopy of the fog. Despite a burning sun, the fog lingered until the last boat was out of range. Fortunately, God was able to lead General Washington and the Continental Army to victory.

We need to recover the truth about who we are and why we exist as a nation. Did God have a plan for America? Was America actually a divine experiment? You bet! We are to be the living proof, as a witness to the rest of the world, that it is possible for a different society to develop on this earth. God can take ordinary people, just like you and me, and He can transform their lives individually. He can then construct a new society based upon the principles of His Word.

As a whole, we Americans have forgotten this. It is the main reason we are in so much trouble today. America is out of balance.

Sir Arnold Toynbee was perhaps the greatest of all world historians. He was once asked the question: "What would you say should be the epitaph to be written of the twentieth century?" Out of his immense knowledge and learning, Dr. Toynbee replied: "Well, I believe I would cause to have written upon the gravestone of this century these words: 'A god in technology; an ape in life.'"

In technology, we are like gods. We are the most technological and scientific society in the world. I marveled as Pathfinder approached Mars. It is sending back incredible pictures and data about the red planet. We can send messages around the world in one-tenth of a second. We have telescopes so powerful and accurate that they can pick up a birthday-candle light 15,500 miles away! We have the greatest medical facilities and care in the world.

However, when it comes to life and daily living we are like "apes." Teenage alcoholism is rampant. Drug abuse threatens to rip apart the fabric of our society. Teenage pregnancies are no longer unusual. Over twenty percent of our high school students carry weapons to school. Violent crimes such as arrests for murder, robbery and aggravated assault under the age of eighteen have increased fifty-four percent during a five-year period. One out of three women will be a victim of rape and/or assault in her lifetime.

In addition to having the highest crime rate in the world, our society has become an amoral society. "Amoral" simply means without morals. Why is this prevalent today? Because the slogan, "If it feels good, then do it," is viewed by the majority of Americans as the only norm for morality. Whatever is normal behavior in society, whatever is relative now, is considered as "right behavior." From media and movies, we are bombarded with the logic that "if it is wrong for you but right for others, then who are you to say it is wrong for them?" There is no appeal whatsoever to God's scriptural standard of morality and ethics.

Is restoration possible? Absolutely! It is not too late, but we have been asleep too long in the light. We must wake up. The key is found in 2 Chronicles 7:14: "If My people who are called by My name will humble themselves, and pray and seek My face, and turn from their wicked ways, then I will hear from heaven, and will forgive their sin and heal their land."

Whether two thousand years ago or two hundred years ago or today, we all must realize our inadequacy, short-sightedness and self-centeredness. We must realize that we have all fallen short of the glory of God. We have blown it! Without accepting this truth, there can be no repentance, and without repentance there can be no forgiveness of sins.

God's mercy and grace are always available if we, His people, will put into practice 2 Chronicles 7:14. Here is the remedy for our nation. As God's people, we as a nation, a community, and church must humble ourselves and pray and seek God's will and turn from our wicked ways. Only then will our nation experience the forgiveness and healing that God alone can give.

This is the linchpin to God's plan for America: that we see ourselves, individually and corporately, in a state of continuing need of God's forgiveness, mercy and grace. It all begins at the foot of the cross.

Early in the nineteenth century the French statesman, Alexis de Tocqueville, made a study of democracy in our country. Here is what he wrote:

> I sought for the greatness and genius of America in her commodious harbors and her ample rivers, and it was not there.

I sought for the greatness and genius of America in her fertile fields and boundless forests, and it was not there.

I sought for the greatness and genius of America in her rich mines and her vast world commerce, and it was not there.

I sought for the greatness and genius of America in her public school system and her institutions of learning, and it was not there.

I sought for the greatness and genius of America in her democratic congress and her matchless constitution, and it was not there.

Not until I went into the churches of America and heard her pulpits flame with righteousness did I understand the secret of her genius and power.

America is great because America is good, and if America ever ceases to be good, America will cease to be great.

There is a divine calling upon America. Peter Marshall is right on target: America was a divine experiment to prove that the gospel of Jesus Christ actually works. We are to be living proof that God can take ordinary sinners, saved by His grace, and build a new society through His love and grace. The result will be a place where people can live together in liberty, justice and peace. America, where will you be when you get where you're going?

Chapter 3

If Your Tomorrow Were Canceled?

In those days Hezekiah was sick and near death. And Isaiah the prophet, the son of Amoz, went to him and said to him, "Thus says the LORD: Set your house in order, for you shall die and not live."
Then Hezekiah turned his face toward the wall, and prayed to the LORD, and said, "Remember now, O LORD, I pray, how I have walked before You in truth and with a loyal heart, and have done what is good in Your sight." And Hezekiah wept bitterly.
And the word of the LORD came to Isaiah, saying, "Go and tell Hezekiah, 'Thus says the LORD, the God of David your father: "I have heard your prayer, I have seen your tears; surely I will add to your days fifteen years"'" (Isaiah 38:1-5).

I magine this scenario: It is evening and you have just finished supper. You decide to relax for a few moments in your favorite chair. You are with friends or family and you tune in to watch your favorite television show. Suddenly, right in the middle of the telecast, you hear the voice from the news center of the network saying, "We interrupt this program to bring you a very important announcement. Your tomorrow has been canceled."

"How ridiculous," you say. "You can't be serious! Why, that's preposterous!" But is it really? I asked one of our church members what she would do if she knew that tomorrow had been canceled. She replied, "I'd be broke!"

Seriously, what if your tomorrow were canceled? What would you do with your life today? What changes would you make in your priorities? What amends would you offer in your relationships? What adjustments would you make in your attitudes? This kind of announcement comes to thousands of persons in the course of every week, everywhere.

We ought to live with the realization that our plans, our lives, and our tomorrows are not certain. There is no guarantee from one day to the next. The only certainty we have about life is the life we have today. On the surface, what seems to be so reliable is the coming of tomorrow. But what if tomorrow were really canceled?

Unfortunately, many in our society have bought into an Epicurean philosophy about life: "Eat, drink, be merry today. For tomorrow you shall die." However, according to God's Word this is deceptive living.

If we attach ourselves too closely to this world and its desires, then somehow we get detached from God and drift away from Him. If we become too enamoured of our possessions to the point where they possess us, then we become friends with the world, which can so easily evolve into enmity toward God.

Who reminds us of this stark reality? In the Old Testament it is King Hezekiah. He, unlike his father King Ahaz, was a good king. But Hezekiah was somewhat like Peter in the New Testament. His life was a blended mixture of faith and impatience.

Isaiah the prophet announced to King Hezekiah, "Set your house in order. Get your estate together. You are not going to live. You are going to die." The king's tomorrow had been canceled. Upon hearing this news, Hezekiah wept bitterly. This was not what he was used to hearing. He was the king. He was a wealthy man. He was well-liked by his countrymen. The king was accustomed to getting his way.

Hezekiah did not want to leave his kingdom or this world. He prayed, "Lord, I've walked in your light. I've followed your statutes. I've been your servant for many years." Then in a beautiful verse of Scripture, the Lord responded to the king's plea, "Hezekiah, I've seen your tears and I've heard your prayers." God answered the king's prayer and sent Isaiah back to Hezekiah. This time the message to the king was good news: God would add fifteen years to his life.

I deal with a lot of folks who get an extension on their lives. Through heart bypasses, organ transplants and other developments in the exploding technology of modern medicine, many have received a few more years of earthly life. A lot of times, I hear people say, "If I ever get out of this predicament, I'm going to change my life. I'm going to live differently." Too often, this kind of commitment is short-lived. It is the Hezekiah syndrome.

Hezekiah started out well. He held a praise gathering and promised to sing God's praises for the rest of his life. But it didn't last very long. It was short-lived and then he was back to business as usual.

Isaiah warned the well-intentioned Hezekiah not to make impetuous alliances with other nations. Hezekiah listened and obeyed. The nation was miraculously spared. However, Hezekiah's impulsiveness sowed the seeds of Jerusalem's destruction. The king received envoys and gifts from the king of Babylon. As a result, Hezekiah blatantly displayed all of the nation's treasures to the Babylonian ambassadors. One hundred thirty years later Isaiah's prophecy of the destruction of Jerusalem and the Babylonian exile were literally fulfilled.

What if you had a guarantee? Let's say tomorrow is not canceled. How are you going to live? Are you going to stay on the same track tomorrow? Are you living as if this were the only life that will ever be?

Are you going to ask God to help you change the direction of your life today? Why are you waiting for another day? Are you living with the conviction that another life awaits beyond this world, and that what happens in this life will ultimately determine your destiny in the next?

This is how we live. We say to ourselves, "I won't worry about that today; I'll take care of it tomorrow. I'll write that book. I'll finish that project. I'll make that commitment. I'll right that wrong." All of this presumes that our tomorrows will not be canceled.

While on a summer vacation, my wife and I took the "Ghostwalk Tour" in Charleston, South Carolina. We walked through some of the oldest cemeteries in the city. The artwork on some of the tombstones clearly depicts that death is a part of life. One of the oldest cemeteries is located in the yard of The Circular Church. One grave is that of a child who died in the eighteenth century. Etched onto the tombstone was the image of a little boy between two symbols, an hourglass and a skull. The boy leans on the skull while looking at the hourglass. I inquired about the intended message of these symbols. The historian replied, "Pay close attention to life—it will soon be over!"

The apostle James also reminds us of this reality. He writes, "You do not know what will happen tomorrow. For what is your life? It is even a vapor that appears for a little time and then vanishes away" (4:14).

We are not told much about James in the New Testament, although he was the brother of Jesus. But he must have had an amazing transformation. At one time he did not believe his brother, Jesus, was the long-awaited Messiah. But somewhere along the way, he, like many others, realized Messiah had come.

James is quick to caution us: "If the Lord wills, we shall live and we shall do this or that." He ends this passage with an interesting verse, "Anyone, then, who knows the right thing to do and fails to do it, commits sin" (4:17, NRSV).

James distinguishes between the sins of commission and the sins of omission. The sins of commission are those things we ought not to do, but do anyway. The sins of omission are those things we know we ought to do, but fail to do them. Let's take a closer look at these two categories of sin.

Sins of Commission

What if tomorrow were canceled and you were not able to take care of the wrong that has been trailing you? This is why one of God's favorite words is "today." "Now is the accepted time; today is the day of salvation." We naturally presume that we will have a tomorrow. We say to ourselves, "Well, I'll take care of it then," but God says, "Don't put it off, do it now; get help for that problem; repent of that sin; confront that situation; join a small discipleship group; open your heart to Christ; spend quality time in prayer; firm up that commitment. Do it! Tomorrow might be canceled."

Saint Augustine understood how we should not be presumptuous toward God or tomorrow when he said, "God has promised us forgiveness for our repentance, but God has not promised us a tomorrow in which to repent."

Sins of Omission

Think of all the good, the right and loving things you intend to do. All the loving acts of mercy, kindness, mission and good intentions. We presume that we will have a tomorrow in which to do those things. But what if tomorrow is canceled? What if all the good things you wanted to say or do for your spouse never got said or done? What about all the loving actions toward your neighbors, friends or church? What about all the loving affections that you plan for your children? Or your parents? But what if tomorrow is canceled?

How prone we are to forget that this world is not our final destination. It is not going to last forever. Time is fleeting! John wrote, "This world and all its desires is passing away. But, they who do the will of God will abide forever" (1 John 2:17). That may be what Augustine meant when he said, "Outside the will of God there is only death."

A soldier finally coming home from Vietnam called his parents from San Francisco. "Mom and Dad, I'm coming home, but I've a favor to ask. I have a friend I'd like to bring with me."

"Sure," they replied, "we'd love to meet him."

"There's something you should know," the son continued, "he was hurt pretty badly in the fighting. He stepped on a land mind and lost an arm and a leg. He has nowhere else to go, and I want him to come live with us."

"I'm sorry to hear that, son. Maybe we can help him find somewhere to live."

"No, Mom and Dad, I want him to live with us."

"Son," said the father, "you don't know what you're asking. Someone with such a handicap would be a terrible burden on us. We have our own lives to live, and we can't let something like this interfere with our lives. I think you should just come home and forget about this guy. He'll find a way to live on his own."

At that point, the son hung up the phone. The parents heard nothing more from him. A few days later, however, they received a call from the San Francisco police. Their son had died after falling from a high building. The police believed it was suicide. The grief-stricken parents flew to San Francisco and were taken to the city morgue to identify the body of their son. They recognized him, but to their horror they also discovered something they didn't know. Their son had been wounded in Vietnam. He had only one arm and one leg. The tomorrow they thought they had with their son had been canceled.

The parents in this story are like many of us. We find it easy to love those who are good-looking or fun-loving, but we do not like people who inconvenience us or make us feel uncomfortable. We would rather stay away from people who are not so healthy, beautiful or smart as we are.

Be thankful that God will not treat us that way. Our heavenly Father loves us with an unconditional love that welcomes us into the forever family, regardless of how messed up we are.

Look over your life today, every goal, every ambition. Is it in Christ? Check out every relationship. Is it in Christ? Does it glorify God? Are all the good works we do in His name and truly for His glory?

What if tomorrow is canceled for you? Today is the day to do what we must do. Now is the time. If tomorrow is canceled and you are in Christ, then the day after tomorrow has been planned for you. If tomorrow is canceled and you are not in Christ, then today is the day of salvation for you. Where will you be when you get where you're going . . . if your tomorrow is canceled?

Chapter 4

Are You a Promise Keeper?

[Jesus said,] "A man had two sons, and he came to the first and said, 'Son, go, work today in my vineyard.' He answered and said, 'I will not,' but afterward he regretted it and went. Then he came to the second and said likewise. And he answered and said, 'I go, sir,' but he did not go. Which of the two did the will of his father?"
They said to Him, "The first."
Jesus said to them, "Assuredly, I say to you that tax collectors and harlots enter the kingdom of God before you. For John came to you in the way of righteousness, and you did not believe him; but tax collectors and harlots believed him; and when you saw it, you did not afterward relent and believe him" (Matthew 21:28-32).

. . . .

Promise Keepers is a Christian movement that has taken the country by storm. Founder Bill McCartney is a former head football coach of the University of

Colorado. This fast-growing organization has generated a great deal of press recently, and not just in the Christian media. They have been featured in *Time, Sports Illustrated,* and many other major publications. The group is aimed specifically at men. The purpose is to challenge men to keep a series of promises that are fundamental to responsible Christian living.

Promise Keepers has touched a nerve and met a need in the Christian community. At no other time in history has the need been greater for Christians to take a stand and live by their convictions. Of course, this does not apply just to men, but to everyone.

Making a promise is easy. Keeping a promise is tough. That's why we should take our promises seriously. We live in a society of broken promises and optional vows. Be careful not to make empty promises. God is calling us to be faithful to the promises we have made: the promise you made to your spouse when you took your marriage vows; the promise you made when you stood at the altar of the church to uphold the church by your prayers, presence, gifts and service; the promise you made at your child's baptism to raise them in the Christian faith and the church.

God is calling us to raise His standard of holy living in this generation, regardless of gender or age. In this parable, Jesus teaches why Christians should be promise keepers. Jesus sets before us an image of two imperfect types of people. The ideal son would be the son who accepted the father's orders with obedience and respect, and fully carried them out. Yet, neither son in the story was the kind of son to bring joy to his father. The behavior of both sons was unsatisfactory. But in the end the one who obeyed was better than the one who made a promise and did not keep it. Three truths emerge from this parable for Christians today.

Good Intentions Aren't Good Enough

First, good intentions are not good enough. In verse 30 the father told one of his sons to go work in the vineyard. The son promised he would but he never did. We are not told why the son never made it to the vineyard. The bottom line is that the reason doesn't matter. All that matters is that he said he would do it, and he did not. He made a promise but did not keep it.

A sick man endured a long hospitalization. His doctor told him, "You are very sick, but you'll pull through." However, the patient was scared for his life. "Please, doctor," he said, "do everything you can. If I get well, I'll donate $10,000 to the building campaign for the new hospital."

Several months later the doctor met the patient on the street and asked him how he felt. The man told the doctor that he felt great. "Good!" the doctor said, "because I have been meaning to speak to you about that donation for the new hospital." The man said, "What are you talking about?" The doctor told him, "You said that if you got well, you would donate $10,000 to the new hospital fund."

The man shook his head. "If I said that, then I must have really been sick!"

You have heard the saying, "The road to hell is paved with good intentions," in which there is much truth. We often deceive ourselves into thinking that good intentions are good enough. We tend to take comfort in the fact that we mean well, even though we don't always do well.

You may want to spend more time with your children. Unfortunately, this does not happen because you spend too much time at the office. You may want to be a tither rather than a tipper, but you never get around to it because you are strapped with too many monthly bills and payments. You may want to spend more time reading the Bible and praying, but time slips away because your hectic schedule consumes too many hours. Thus, your good intentions have not helped you or others at all.

A young associate pastor was serving his first church. He was given his big chance to participate in the morning worship service. It was Mother's Day. He was to read the lesson from Second Timothy where Paul writes, "I have been reminded of your sincere faith, which first lived in your grandmother Lois and in your mother Eunice and, I am persuaded, now lives in you also" (1:5, NIV). When the young minister stepped into the pulpit he began by saying, "I would like to dedicate this Scripture reading to all the ladies of our congregation," and he began to read. Unfortunately, he did not read from the first chapter of Second Timothy. He read from First Timothy chapter one, and this is what he said: "Some of you have wandered away from the faith and have turned to meaningless talk. You want to be teachers but you do not know what you are talking about" (vv. 6-7, free translation). Needless to say, his efforts were not appreciated. Shortly after this happened, the young minister received a call to go to the mission field.

Our Walk Is More Important than Our Talk

Second, our walk is more important than our talk. There are those people whose profession is much better than their practice. They will promise anything. They make grandiose statements about their spirituality, but their practice lags far behind.

The life of Mahatma Gandhi was amazing. He was not a professing Christian, and he never claimed to be. But Gandhi did commit to live his life according to the teachings of Jesus. He specifically attempted to pattern his life after the Sermon on the Mount. In some ways, he lived a better life than some professing Christians.

This parable teaches that religious talk is not enough. Look at verse 31, "Which of the two did the will of his

Father?" It was not the one who said he would work in the vineyard but did not. It was the one who said he would not go, but ended up going anyway. He may not have said the right thing, but he did the right thing.

Our walk is more important than our talk! Profession and practice need to meet and match. It is not enough simply to say that we believe the right things about God. If our actions and lifestyles do not back up our words, our words are meaningless. This truth is emphasized repeatedly throughout Scripture, as in James's letter: "For just as the body without the spirit is dead, so faith without works is also dead" (2:26 NRSV).

Francis Bacon said that it is not so much what we preach and say, but what we practice and believe that makes a difference in the Christian life. Saint Francis of Assisi said, "Preach the gospel at all times, and when necessary use words." This is what Jesus was saying in this parable: A promise can never take the place of performance. It is what we *do,* and not just what we say that ultimately makes the difference in our lives and in the lives of others.

Who You Are Today Is What Counts

Third, who you are today is more important than who you were yesterday. Years before the time of Christ, the Pharisees were determined to revitalize Judaism, and they were successful. Their revival had a major impact on early Jewish thought. However, the Pharisees did not keep the promise they made to obey God. Eventually, their intense passion was replaced by coldhearted legalism. The Pharisees embellished the Old Testament law to the point that no one could keep it. In the process, their love for God began to grow cold.

On the other hand, the tax collectors, the harlots and other sinners were those who said they would go their own way. They lived life "doing their thing." Then they heard

Jesus' message of salvation. Jesus proclaimed: "The king-dom of God is here . . . right now . . . in your midst . . . and you can have a relationship with God today. No matter who you are or what you've done . . . no matter what your past is like . . . God will heal and forgive. God will give you eternal life today!"

The tax collectors and harlots turned from living their way to God's way. The Christian life can be described like this: "I'm not what I ought to be, but I'm not what I used to be, and I'm not yet what I'm going to be."

The difference between the two brothers in the parable is that one was a talker and one was a walker. It is not so much what you say that really counts, it is what you do. Good intentions are not good enough. Our walk is more important than our talk. God and His church, your family and friends are counting on you.

In 1966, while he was unemployed and aimlessly drifting, the former Notre Dame coach Lou Holtz listed on paper 107 lifetime ambitions. Becoming head coach of the Notre Dame Fighting Irish fulfilled one of those goals. Winning a national championship fulfilled another. Other goals on the list included dinner at the White House, a guest appearance on "The Tonight Show" and ownership of a 1949 Chevrolet. Almost all of his goals have been realized by now. Lou Holtz's advice is simple: "Don't be a spectator, and don't let life pass you by."

Where will you be when you get where you're going . . . by making promises and keeping them?

Chapter 5

Staying Alive

But God, who is rich in mercy, because of His great love with which He loved us, even when we were dead in trespasses, made us alive together with Christ (by grace you have been saved), and raised us up together, and made us sit together in the heavenly places in Christ Jesus, that in the ages to come He might show the exceeding riches of His grace in His kindness toward us in Christ Jesus. For by grace you have been saved through faith, and that not of yourselves; it is the gift of God, not of works, lest anyone should boast. For we are His workmanship, created in Christ Jesus for good works, which God prepared beforehand that we should walk in them (Ephesians 2:4-10).

. . . .

In the mid 1970s American disco music and dancing replaced the British pop sounds of the Beatles, the Rolling Stones, and the Who. Actor John Travolta was one of the main reasons. With his twisting, turning and moving to the beat on the disco floor, he quickly rose to stardom with two hit movies, *Saturday Night Fever* and *Staying Alive.* In the latter movie, Travolta was attempting to stay alive in spite of all his personal difficulties and emerging competition from others. Regardless of these distractions, he stayed focused and was able, against all odds, to stay alive in the disco world.

Some clergy were discussing the issue of when life begins. "Life begins," said the Catholic, "at the moment of conception." "No, no, Father," said the Presbyterian. "Life begins at the moment of birth." Both of them turned to the aging rabbi and asked, "Well, what do you think?" Slowly stroking his beard, the rabbi said, "Life begins . . . life begins when the kids leave home and the dog dies."

It is often said that life really begins at forty. I am not going to argue that point. Another generally held belief is that life is over when one reaches retirement. Now, that does not leave many years in between. Life, real life, can begin whenever you want it to begin, and it can go on and on—regardless of age. It is not just living but staying alive for the rest of your life that really counts. How can you stay alive for the rest of your life?

God Accepts You

First, know that God accepts you as a person of infinite worth. You are uniquely valuable to God. Before the world was even created, God had you in His infinite mind. God has scheduled each day for each person. The psalmist said, "Your eyes saw my substance, being yet unformed. And in Your book they all were written, The days fashioned for me, When as yet there were none of them" (139:16). This is why "abortion on demand" is so tragic. It interrupts the eternal plan of God for the individual person.

Unfortunately, our value as persons is often measured by what we do or by how much we make or accomplish or produce. Our value to God is based not on what we do but on who we are. We are created in God's image. All human beings are valuable to God.

John McKay was the former football coach at the University of Southern California. McKay's son was a successful player on his dad's team. When asked to comment on the pride he felt for his son's accomplishments on the field, McKay answered, "I'm pleased that my son had a good season last year. He does a fine job and I am proud of him. But I would be just as proud of him if he had never played the game at all."

Coach McKay teaches us a good lesson. His son's football talent is recognized and appreciated, but his human worth does not depend on his ability to play football. Human worth is more than accomplishment, position or production. Your worth to God is beyond human calculation. You are God's most valuable resource in His kingdom! Your infinite worth to God will help you stay alive for the rest of your life.

God Has a Purpose for Your Life

Second, know that God has a purpose for your life. Since you are a person of infinite worth, God has a purpose for your being. Knowing God's purpose and dream will help you stay alive the rest of your life. God revealed to Jeremiah that the future purpose for His people already had His blessing. "I know the thoughts that I think toward you, says the LORD, thoughts of peace and not of evil, to give you a future and a hope" (29:11).

Centuries ago, God said to Joshua that the Promised Land would belong to him and the children of Israel, but they would have to go and possess it. God is saying the same thing to each one of us: "I have a plan for your life. I have a dream for this world, and you are a significant part of this dream."

Frequently, the difference between the person who *enjoys* life and the person who *endures* life is that the former dreamed big dreams and set goals to reach them. Stephen Covey wrote a bestselling book entitled *The Seven Habits of Highly Effective People.* A basic premise in his book is that we should begin with the end in mind and keep our eyes fixed there.

Unfortunately, too many people are like the hero of the *Marvin* comic strip. Marvin is heard to say, "I think it's important to establish goals in life. I've set both short-term and long-term goals for myself." As he sucks on his bottle, he explains, "My short-term goal is to get fed again in four hours. My long-term goal is to get fed again in eight hours."

Too many of us are aiming no higher than Marvin. We are interested only in instant gratification. We are interested only in the short-term. We have no long-term goals or plans for our lives.

The nearest thing to death is when there is no meaning or purpose toward which to strive and stretch. Purpose, not wealth or success, makes life worthwhile. Life is tragic for the person who has plenty to live on but nothing to live for.

Without dreams and a purpose for your life, your life is like a ship without a rudder. If you have no dreams, then you have no direction for your life. Whatever you do, keep your dreams alive. The apostle Paul said, "Do all things to the glory of God" (1 Corinthians 10:31). The point is this: If you always do what you have always done, you'll always be what you've always been. We may not be able to do all we want to do, but that should not keep us from doing the things we can do.

Develop a Positive Attitude

Third, develop a positive attitude. In the past fifty years, more has been written on this subject than in any other period of history. Norman Vincent Peale and Robert Schuller brought it to the forefront of religious groups. If God's purpose for your life is like the rudder of the ship, then your attitude determines the direction of the ship. A biblical proverb states, "As [a man] thinks in his heart, so is he" (Proverbs 23:7). Paul said, "Be transformed by the renewing of your mind, that you may prove what is that good and acceptable and perfect will of God" (Romans 12:2).

Some people have a difficult time developing a positive attitude. Nothing is ever right for them. The world is a bad place to live. They see nothing good in anyone. They are like the farmer who was always complaining about the insects or the weather or the low prices at the market. Then a year came when all the conditions were favorable and he produced a bumper crop. "Well, you have it made now," said a friend. The farmer replied, "But a harvest like this is pretty hard on the soil." For some people, nothing will ever be right.

Viktor Frankl left his mark upon the world as one of this century's greatest psychiatrists. At his death, he was the leading professor of psychiatry at the University of Vienna. In his book, *Man's Search for Meaning,* he described his experiences in Hitler's concentration camps. He wrote, "We who lived in concentration camps can remember the men who walked through the huts comforting others, giving away their last piece of bread. They have been few in number, but they offer sufficient proof that everything can be taken from a man but one thing: the last of the human freedoms—to choose one's attitude in any given set of circumstances . . . Anyone who has a 'why' to live can endure almost any 'how.'" According to Frankl, the people who survived that terrible ordeal had maintained a positive outlook on life. Not only did they have something of substance in their life that gave them meaning, but also their positive attitude helped to keep them alive.

Our attitude is the mirror of our minds. We are the reflection of our thoughts. The apostle Paul wrote to the Philippian church, "Whatever is true, whatever is honorable, whatever is just, whatever is pure, whatever is pleasing, whatever is commendable, if there is any excellence and if there is anything worthy of praise, think about these things" (4:8, NRSV). A positive attitude will help us stay alive for the rest of our lives.

Give Your Life Away

Fourth, give your life away to a cause greater than yourself. We have heard the Scripture many times, "It is more blessed to give than to receive" (Acts 20:35). Life comes to us when we give it away. Mother Teresa literally gave her life away to the poor and disenfranchised of Calcutta, India. For grace to abound, our giving should be sacrificial, and maybe even seem a little reckless.

Jesus was visiting in Bethany, a small village outside Jerusalem. A woman rushed into the house, broke an alabaster jar, and poured all the contents on the Master's feet. It certainly was not a planned event. It was a spontaneous moment of giving. It was a burst of emotion born out of love. In one sense, it was reckless giving.

A college president had an old wooden turtle on his desk. It seemed out of place in a college president's office. Everyone who came to see him asked about it. He would hold it up for them to read the inscription on the bottom. It said: "Remember the turtle. He makes progress only when he sticks his neck out."

Jesus said, "For whoever desires to save his life will lose it, but whoever loses his life for My sake will find it" (Matthew 16:25). If you want to stay alive for the rest of your life, you have to give your life away to Jesus Christ and His kingdom.

God Is with You

Finally, remember that God is with you. God sent His Son into the world so that we might live abundantly—not just hereafter, but here and now. Jesus said, "I have come that they may have life, and that they may have it more abundantly" (John 10:10). Jesus came to empower us with His Spirit to live a meaningful and full life.

Paderewski was one of the world's leading pianists. At one of his concerts, the crowd anxiously awaited his arrival. A nine-year-old boy grew impatient with all the waiting but was fascinated by the Steinway grand piano on stage. The boy slipped away from his parents to explore the beautiful instrument. Oblivious to the crowd in the concert hall, he sat down at the piano and began to play "Chopsticks."

The crowd was stunned. Some laughed, others cried out in anger, and some yelled for the ushers to take him out. Backstage, Paderewski looked out to see about the noise and saw the young lad sitting where he was soon to be. He quickly went out, took his seat beside the young boy, and began playing a beautiful counter harmony. The master pianist then whispered in the boy's ear, "Don't stop . . . just keep playing!"

That is what Jesus Christ does for us. He came to be with us, and He is still with us! He speaks to us His own words, "Lo, I am with you always" (Matthew 28:20). Though the music of our lives may be incomplete, or somewhat out of tune, Jesus desires to make something beautiful out of it. With Christ, you can stay alive for the rest of your life, which will last forever.

Where will you be when you get where you're going . . . by staying alive for the rest of your life?

Chapter 6

Giving Beyond Our Ability

[W]e make known to you the grace of God bestowed on the churches of Macedonia: that in a great trial of affliction the abundance of their joy and their deep poverty abounded to the riches of their liberality. For I bear witness that according to their ability, yes, and beyond their ability, they were freely willing, imploring us with much urgency that we would receive the gift and the fellowship of the ministering to the saints. And not only as we had hoped, but they first gave themselves to the Lord, and then to us by the will of God. So we urged Titus, that as he had begun, so he would also complete this grace in you as well. But as you abound in everything—in faith, in speech, in knowledge, in all diligence, and in your love for us—see that you abound in this grace also (2 Corinthians 8:1-7).

We sometimes hear the statement, "Money talks." It really is true. You can tell things about people when you learn how they earn their money and where they spend it. You discover motives, standards, desires, and the depth of their Christian commitment.

One day Herman and Clara were riding along in their shiny new car. Clara spoke up and said, "You know, Herman, if it were not for my money, we probably wouldn't have this wonderful new car." Herman just sat there and didn't say a word. They pulled into their driveway, and Herman turned off the engine. As they quietly admired their beautiful home, Clara said, "You know, Herman, if it were not for my money, we probably wouldn't have this house." Herman just sat there and didn't say a word. That afternoon a delivery truck pulled up in front of the house, and the men delivered a new grand piano. It was placed in the living room where its shiny finish caught the rays of the sun. Clara said, "You know, Herman, if it were not for my money, we probably wouldn't have this piano." Once more, Herman just sat there and didn't say a word.

Later that night, Herman and Clara went to bed. As they pulled up the covers on the bed, Clara paused and in a reflective mood said, "You know, Herman, if it were not for my money, we wouldn't have this warm comfortable bed." With that, poor old Herman turned to Clara and said, "You know, Clara, if it were not for your money I wouldn't be here either!"

A careful investigation of the New Testament reveals that one-third of all Jesus' parables and one-sixth of all His teachings had to do with money and material possessions. To follow Jesus in a preaching and teaching ministry would literally mean that one-third of a pastor's sermons should deal with Christian stewardship. This means seventeen Sundays out of fifty-two would be dedicated to this topic!

Jesus approached life from the perspective that everything belongs to God. We are simply stewards and managers of what God has given us. How we manage what we have been given and what we do with it reveals not only the direction in which our lives are headed but also the character of who we are. Someone has said, "If you do what you can with what you have where you are, then God will not leave you where you are and He will bless what you have."

Where will you be when you get where you're going with what you have?

Two matters are striking about 2 Corinthians 8. One is that Paul tells us about people in a church who actually begged to give more money to do God's work! Can you believe that? They were certainly not average church members. Few of us beg to give more money to the church. We usually have to be prodded and challenged. We have to have clever campaigns in order to raise funds for ministries and missions.

The churches of Macedonia were the churches located in northern Greece; namely, Philippi, Thessalonica and Berea. The Macedonians had given so generously and liberally that they became a model of stewardship for the Corinthian church as well as for the church today.

The other striking feature here is that Paul indicates he is trying to find out how genuine the Corinthian's love is for God. The only tangible measure of their faithfulness was revealed by what they were giving. In other words, Paul determines how much the Corinthians love Christ by correlation to what they give. In essence, Paul argues that we prove our love for Christ by the motive and quality of our giving.

The Level of Obligation

Christians may follow three levels of giving. First, there is the level of obligation. We give because we feel that it is our duty. We feel it is our obligation, like paying weekly or monthly dues. If this is the level of our giving, then we are simply paying for the benefits of our Christian religion.

In 2 Samuel, David took a census of the people. The pride thus exhibited made God angry. David repented and accepted the blame for it. When he did, a prophet came with a word from God. David was to build an altar on the threshing floor of a Jebusite to show his repentance. So David sent a messenger to a Jebusite man and offered to buy the threshing floor. The man was honored by the request of his king and begged him to take the floor as a gift. But David would not do it. He said, "I will surely buy it from you for a price; nor will I offer burnt offerings to the LORD my God with that which cost me nothing" (24:25). David felt an obligation to give an offering to God. He did not look for the shortcut or the easy way out of his obligation.

His attitude was much different from that of a certain family as they drove home after a Sunday morning worship service. Dad thought the sermon was terrible, Mom was criticizing the choir, and their daughter thought the hymns were dragging. Then little Johnny piped up and said, "But it was a pretty good show for a dollar, wasn't it, Dad?"

Ancient Jews believed the tithe, which means "tenth," was a kind of income tax payable to the "Department of Eternal Revenue." There was nothing to shout or feel proud about if one paid it. The tithe simply belonged to God. It was an obligation for every faithful Jewish person to pay. Anything above this was generosity. We who live on this side of the Cross sometimes feel that we can give God His due with our spare time and whatever is leftover after buying the "necessities of life."

If we belong to a club or union, we pay dues, and we expect to. If we go to a doctor, we pay a bill and we expect to. If we invest in a house, we make monthly installments on the mortgage and we expect to. But the church is one of the few, if not the only place, where many expect to receive benefits free.

The Level of Generosity

The second level of giving is generosity. This is the level beyond our obligation as members. John Wesley, father of Methodism, once preached a sermon that had three good points. "Earn all you can," was the first point. As one story goes, a boisterous man in the crowd said, "Amen." Wesley preached his second point, "Save all you can." The same man yelled, "Amen." Then Wesley preached his final point, "Give all you can." The man is reported to have said, "What a shame to spoil a good sermon."

Wesley was talking about generosity. He was talking about how we can reach beyond the level of feeling obligated to a generous act of love in our giving.

The church in Jerusalem was passing through a hard time. The Christians were very poor, perhaps because of persecution by the Jews. Paul called on the prosperous Christians at Corinth to help. He did not ask for contributions directly. Instead he told them how generous the churches in Macedonia had been, which was remarkable because the people in Macedonia had been having their own difficulties. The Romans had taxed them until they had almost nothing left. Instead of their hardship making them stingy, it made them give more freely. Somehow their own need made them realize more deeply the needs of others. They went beyond their ability in giving. They asked and even begged to give out of their affliction and poverty to aid Christian brothers and sisters in far-off Jerusalem.

A blacksmith repaired a rake and hoe like new for a farmer. The farmer tried to pay him for the work. But the blacksmith refused to take any pay. The farmer insisted. Then the blacksmith said, "Ed, can't you let a man do something now and then just to stretch his soul?"

Stretching our souls! Just think about it. Stretching our souls in giving for Jesus Christ and His church. What a glorious expression for Christian stewardship.

The Level of Sacrifice

This leads us to the third level of giving, which is the greatest of all: the level of sacrifice. Jesus and His disciples were sitting close to the collection boxes in the temple at Jerusalem. They watched as people put in their offerings. This may be the reason the rich put in their huge sums—for the sake of appearances. Then a certain widow approached the box. She dropped in her two pennies. This was the least that the law allowed, but it was all the poor woman had. Jesus was watching, and He told His disciples she had put in more than all the others. The rest had given out of their abundance, but she had given sacrificially out of her poverty.

There is only one motive to lead a person to give at the level of sacrifice: gratitude for what God has done for us through Jesus Christ.

The Vietnam conflict was a political event. It was a fight that we could not win. In fact that was the determining factor that drove President Lyndon B. Johnson out of office. The disaster left a black mark on American history. When our soldiers came home they were not greeted by ticker-tape parades or yellow ribbons tied around trees to welcomed them. Many heroes and heroines gave their lives in that war. Few were recognized. Fortunately, a black marble wall in Washington, D.C., finally reminds us of those who made the ultimate sacrifice.

One of the heroes was a marine named lieutenant Clebe McCleary. Only two or three weeks after getting married, Lieutenant McCleary went to Vietnam. The commanding officer asked for volunteers to go on "recon duty." In the Marine Corps, if you went on reconnaissance it really meant you had left on a suicide mission. Fifty percent of the soldiers who did so never returned.

Twelve people were dropped behind enemy lines with enough rations to last for about a week. They were to live off the land for another one or two months. Their mission was to monitor troop movement and supply convoys. They were then to radio the location of the enemy forces back to headquarters so that the artillery units could bombard these targets.

Lieutenant McCleary went on eighteen separate missions without any casualties, which was nothing short of a miracle. But on the nineteenth mission at about two o'clock one morning the enemy discovered him and his men. The enemy attacked and surrounded the Americans. Strapping explosives onto their bodies, they jumped into the foxholes, blowing themselves up along with our troops. Lieutenant McCleary was gravely wounded. His left arm was blown off. His left eye was blown out of the socket, and shrapnel shredded the lower extremities of his body.

An air medic helicopter rescued McCleary and the few other survivors. The officer endured 32 surgeries and procedures before his body began to function somewhat as it should. While convalescing in the States, he received a plaque from the troops who survived that terrible battle and remained in Vietnam. These words came from the brave men who fought with Lieutenant McCleary on that dark day:

> To Lieutenant Clebe McCleary, Our Leader! In a world of give and take, there are far too many people who are willing to take and take and take and take. And there are far too few people who are willing to give what it really takes to get the job done. But thanks be to God, for you our leader, who were willing to give all that it took to get the job done. We will never forget you—ever!

It is absolutely amazing what vision and sacrifice can do when they come together. Years ago a thirteen-year-old boy read about Dr. Albert Schweitzer's missionary medical work in Africa. He wanted to help but had only enough money to buy one bottle of aspirin. He wrote the Air Force and asked them to fly his bottle of aspirin to Africa to help Dr. Schweitzer. A radio station broadcast the story and the newspapers picked it up. People from all over the country began to donate medical items and supplies. Eventually, the government flew this young boy to Dr. Schweitzer's hospital, along with four and one-half tons of medical supplies. When we do all we can, God takes our gift and does more.

Every level of giving is good, but at the level of sacrifice, the need becomes so compelling that we give beyond our ability. Where will you be when you get where you're going . . . by living at the level of sacrifice?

Chapter 7

Launch Out into the Deep

*As the multitude pressed about [Jesus] to hear the
word of God . . . He stood by the Lake of Gennesaret,
and saw two boats standing by the lake; but the
fishermen had gone from them and were washing their
nets. Then He got into one of the boats, which was
Simon's, and asked him to put out a little from the
land. And He sat down and taught the multitudes
from the boat.*

*When He had stopped speaking, He said to Simon,
"Launch out into the deep and let down
your nets for a catch."*

*But Simon answered and said to Him, "Master, we
have toiled all night and caught nothing; nevertheless
at Your word I will let down the net." And when they
had done this, they caught a great number of fish, and
their net was breaking. So they signaled to their
partners in the other boat to come and help them. And*

they came and filled both the boats, so that they began
to sink. When Simon Peter saw it, he fell down at
Jesus' knees, saying, "Depart from me,
for I am a sinful man, O Lord!"
For he and all who were with him were astonished at
the catch of fish which they had taken; and so also
were James and John, the sons of Zebedee, who were
partners with Simon. And Jesus said to Simon, "Do
not be afraid. From now on you will catch men." So
when they had brought their boats to land, they
forsook all and followed Him
(Luke 5:1-11).

. . . .

There is an experience of a beach scene recorded in Luke 5. Here we see Peter, James and John fishing along the shore of Lake Gennesaret. They were professional fishermen. They were tired and worn down. They were discouraged and disappointed because they had fished all night and caught nothing.

Jesus was so perceptive. He discerned the situation quickly and saw their problem. Unlike so many, Jesus not only saw their problem but points them to the solution. He said, "You're too shallow! Launch out into the deep and let down your nets!" Peter answered, "But, Master, we have worked all night and have caught nothing. They are not biting. We're ready to quit. But if you say so, we'll give it another try."

They followed Jesus' suggestion and did precisely what He told them to do. They launched out into deep water and let down their nets. And the result? They caught so many fish their nets began to break. There were so many they had to call other boats to help bring in all the fish. Simon Peter was so astonished by the power of the Master that he felt unworthy to be in the presence of such greatness.

He rushed to shore, fell at the feet of Jesus, and cried out, "Depart from me, Lord, for I am a sinful man." But

Jesus lifted Simon Peter up and called him to a life of discipleship: "Come, Simon, and follow me. Do not be afraid; from now on you will be catching people." Simon, James, and John left everything and followed Him.

Many things can be said about this story: the miracle catch, the call to discipleship, the significance of the seashore, the absence of Simon's brother, Andrew. There is the importance of obedience and of doing precisely what the Master tells us to do. There is the sense of unworthiness that Simon felt in the powerful presence of Jesus.

All these things are important, but we need to launch out into the deep and discover the new birth that comes as Christ takes us out of the shallows and into the depths of new life and faith. His word to us in this passage rings loud and clear. Can you hear the Master calling your name, saying, "Launch out into the deep! You've been in the shallows long enough. Push out into the deep and find new life!"

Launch into the Depths of Gratitude

We can launch out into the depths of gratitude. When Simon Peter saw that incredible catch of fish that Christ had blessed them with, he was filled with gratitude. I can hear him saying with the psalmist, "Bless the LORD, O my soul: and all that is within me, bless his holy name. Bless the LORD, O my soul, and forget not all his benefits" (103:1-2, KJV).

This is the song of genuine gratitude, yet so often, the song goes unsung. We have so much to be thankful for, and yet the truth is that we do forget to thank God for His goodness. Too often, we take God's blessing for granted. We just play around in the shallow waters of gratitude.

A woman once said to her doctor, "Doctor, why am I seized with restless longings for the glamorous and the faraway?" The doctor replied, "My dear lady, they are the usual symptoms of too much comfort in the home and too much ingratitude in the heart."

If we want a new lease on life, a new start, a new beginning, a new birth, a new zest, we can find all that in the depths of gratitude. If we will reach out and take Christ's hand, He will lead us into the deeper waters of thankfulness.

Launch into the Depths of Repentance

We can launch out into the depths of repentance. First, Simon Peter felt gratitude. Then he felt penitence. He was so awed and astonished by the amazing power of Jesus that he felt unworthy to be in His presence. Like Moses at the burning bush, he knew he stood on holy ground. Like Isaiah in the temple, he felt he was an unclean man with unclean lips, dwelling in the midst of an unclean people. In anguish, Simon Peter cried out, "Go away from me, Lord, for I am a sinful man."

In the Scriptures, repentance is a painful process, a deeply moving experience. People cry, tear their clothes, fall on their knees and change their ways. But today the truth is that, more often than not, we treat sin lightly. We just play around in the shallow waters of repentance.

A brazen young woman felt she was possessed by seven demons. She was taken before a Roman Catholic priest who was an exorcist. The priest looked at her and said, "I can help you. I can cast out those seven demons. Would you like me to do this for you?" To which the young woman replied, "Would you mind just casting out six?"

Like that woman, something within us wants to hold back. Something inside us tries to keep us from letting go and letting God take over. Often we play around with repentance. It's like swimming in the shallow end.

We are much like the man who became irate when the neighborhood children walked on his freshly poured concrete drive. He went ballistic! Finally, his wife said to him, "Why are you so angry? I thought you loved children."

"I do love children," he said, "but I love them in the abstract, not in the concrete!"

We tend to repent in the abstract; our repentance is not concrete. Repentance means not only being sorry for our sins, but also turning away from our sins to Christ. We stop going in one direction and turn to Christ and move in His direction.

In the New Testament, the Hebrew word for "repent" is "*metanoia*." It literally means "about face," "turn around," "change direction." If we want a new life, a new start, one place to find that new beginning is out there in the depths of repentance. Christ helps us to launch out into the depths of gratitude and into the depths of repentance.

Launch into the Depths of Christian Commitment

Finally, we can launch out into the depths of Christian commitment. Simon, James and John left everything and followed Jesus. Their commitment was so total that they turned the world upside down—or right side up! A shallow commitment is not really worth much at all. A deep commitment is one of the most powerful things in the world.

A young soldier was brought into a field hospital with a badly shattered arm. The surgeon had to amputate at the elbow. When the young soldier came out of the anesthetic, the surgeon told him as gently as he could, "Son, I'm sorry, but we had to take your arm." The soldier, although groggy and weak, was able to say, "Sir, you did not take it. I gave it!" Now, that's commitment.

According to church tradition, the Romans crucified Simon Peter because of his allegiance to Christ. I can imagine Simon Peter telling them, "Crucify me! Crucify me upside down! I am not worthy to be sacrificed like my Lord!" The centurion tells him, "But, Simon, if you will deny Christ right now, we will not have to take your life. You will be spared." Simon Peter answers, "You are not taking my life. I'm giving it!"

This is launching out into the depths of Christian commitment. It is the giving of ourselves in complete devotion to Christ. How deep is your commitment to Christ?

A wealthy British family went to Scotland for a summer vacation. The mother and father looked forward to enjoying the beautiful Scottish countryside with their young son. But one fateful day, the son ventured off and got himself into big trouble. The English youth walked through the Scottish woods and came across an old abandoned swimming hole. To most adults a place like that would have "danger" written on it but to this young boy it looked like fun. So he took off his shoes and shirt and jumped into the water. He was totally unprepared for what happened next. As soon as he hit the water he was seized by a vicious attack of swimmer's cramp. Both of his legs were immobilized. He could not stay afloat. As he was going down he yelled for help. It happened that a young Scottish farm boy was working in a field nearby. He heard the cry for help and came running. He plunged into the deep water and brought the drowning English boy to the bank.

The father of the rescued boy was very grateful. The Scottish farm boy had saved his son's life. The next day the father met with the Scottish lad to thank him for his heroic and sacrificial deed. As they visited, the English father was impressed with the Scottish boy and asked him what he planned to do with his life. The boy answered, "Well, I suppose I will just stay here and be a farmer like my dad."

The English gentleman discerned that the boy was not too excited about his future. He asked him, "Is there something else you would like to do?"

"Oh yes," answered the young Scottish boy. "All my life I have dreamed about being a doctor. But we are too poor and my family has no money to send me to school."

The Englishman said, "Never mind that! If you want to be a doctor you shall have your heart's desire. Make your plans. Go study medicine. And I will take care of all the costs." The grateful Englishman kept his word and paid for everything. In time the young Scottish boy became a doctor.

Years later, in December 1943, Prime Minister Winston Churchill went on a visit to Africa and became seriously ill. It was a grave and precarious situation for this world leader. Word was sent to the noted physician, Sir Alexander Fleming, to come immediately. Dr. Alexander Fleming was the doctor who discovered penicillin. He flew to Africa from England and administered his new drug to the Prime Minister. In doing so, Dr. Fleming saved the life of Winston Churchill—for the second time. Alexander Fleming was the young Scottish farm boy who had plunged into the murky waters of an old abandoned swimming hole in Scotland to save the life of a young English boy who just happened to be Winston Churchill.

This story illustrates in dramatic fashion the principle of launching out into the deep. The young Fleming boy risked his life to save someone else. He heard the call and responded by launching out into the deep to save the life of someone else. He expected nothing in return; he did it because it was the right and loving thing to do. As a result of that unselfish act, his dream became reality and he became a doctor.

Winston Churchill's father gave Fleming his education for only one reason—gratitude—and expected nothing in return. But look how that gift came back to bless the Churchill family. The medical training that he paid for out of gratitude ended up saving his own son's life.

We all need to hear and respond, in faith and obedience, to God's Word for us today. Launch out into the deep. Get out of the shallows. Launch out into the depths of gratitude, repentance and commitment.

Where will you be when you get where you're going . . . by launching out into the deep?

Chapter 8

What Does God Expect from Me?

With what shall I come before the LORD, And bow myself before the High God? Shall I come before Him with burnt offerings, With calves a year old? Will the LORD be pleased with thousands of rams, Ten thousand rivers of oil? Shall I give my firstborn for my transgression, The fruit of my body for the sin of my soul? He has shown you, O man, what is good; And what does the LORD require of you But to do justly, To love mercy, And to walk humbly with your God? (Micah 6:6-8)

. . . .

Every day of walking with Jesus is very special in the life of the Christian. It reminds me of the husband who was getting ready for work. Before he left the house his wife said, "Honey, I'll bet you don't know what today is." He looked at her and said, "Of course, I do! Before the day is over, you'll see that I do know what today is."

He arrived at his office and carefully looked at the calendar. He brought his secretary in and they went over his wife's birthday, their anniversary and all of the children's birthdays. He just could not figure it out. He decided to respond to the occasion anyway. That morning he sent his wife two dozen roses. In the late afternoon, he dropped by a department store and bought his wife her favorite perfume. When he got home that evening, he told her they were going out to celebrate the big day. He took her to the nicest restaurant in town. But he still could not figure it out.

Finally, when they came home that night, he thought he would try one more thing. He looked at his wife and said, "And you thought I didn't know what today was." She said, "Honey, I'll have to admit that this is the greatest Groundhog Day I have ever experienced!"

There are times when we just do not know what God or others are expecting from us. Trying to figure out the right answers can be very frustrating. But have you thought about this: the right *questions* are important, too! How essential it is to match the right answers with the right questions. Nowhere is this more important than in the realm of the Christian faith.

It is common these days to see bumper stickers, posters, lapel buttons and highway signs displaying the words "Faith Is the Answer." Of course, we believe this to be true, but this phrase must be more than a religious cliché. The serious secular thinker will not let us get away with catchy slogans. The serious thinker comes back and asks: "Well, if faith is the answer, then what is the question?"

Math books sometimes have the answers printed in the back of the book. You can always get the right answer there, but answers by themselves mean nothing. They become significant and meaningful only when they are related to specific problems in the text. Only then does learning and growth take place. The question I am asking is simply this: "What does God expect from me?"

Psychologists tell us that as long as we live, we will have two conflicting desires working within us. One desire is the temptation to quit on life, to throw in the towel and give in to boredom and mediocrity. The other desire is the determination and motivation to move forward and to discover God's truth and His will for us.

The question, "What does God expect from me?" helps us to move forward in our Christian walk. In fact, this question is answered in the book of Micah. It is one of the highest mountain peaks in all Scripture.

The prophet Micah sees that much of the religion of his day had gotten off track. The people were doing all kinds of religious things. They were going to the temple on a regular basis. They were burning incense, lighting candles, paying tithes and even offering sacrifices. Then as now, much of their religiosity was not impacting their lifestyle.

They had a form of religion but it was not a factor in daily life. They separated worship on the Sabbath from their lifestyle on the six other days. Micah tells us that God expects three things from us.

Do What Is Right

First, God expects us to do what is right. We are called to do the right thing, to do justice. In the Scripture, the word for "justice" means "righteousness." It means "doing what is right." But it also means working for what is just and right in our society.

Several years ago in Ohio, the back door of an armored truck came open and two million dollars flew out the back. Can you imagine that? It was raining hundred-dollar bills on the highway. Motorists stopped and grabbed all the money they could get their hands on. They stuffed money in bags and sacks and sped away. One man picked up fifty-seven thousand dollars. He turned the exact amount in to the authorities the next day. He indicated to the police that he could not sleep. It was not his money and he could not keep it with a clear conscience. He was one of the few who felt that way. Of the two million dollars lost, only a very small percentage was returned; most of that was by this one man.

When questioned by a reporter the man's father said, "What? He gave it back? I thought my son was smarter than that. I didn't do a very good job of raising that boy. How stupid can you be?" But the man's mother said, "We sure could have used that money, but I'm so proud of him. It was the right thing to do."

To do justice means to do the right thing.

Love Mercy

Second, God expects us to love mercy. We are called to be merciful to other people. Jesus said, "Blessed are the merciful, For they shall obtain mercy" (Matthew 5:7).

A young man in Napoleon's army committed a deed so terrible that it was worthy of death. The day before he was scheduled to go before the firing squad, the young man's mother went to Napoleon and pleaded for mercy for her son. Napoleon replied, "Woman, your son does not deserve mercy."

"I know," she answered, "If he deserved it, it would not be mercy."

In the early days of Oral Roberts University, a young student struggled academically and especially with the strict discipline. He repeatedly broke the rules of campus life. The school counselors felt that there was no other recourse but to expel him from school. The young man was sent to President Roberts, who told the student that he would have to leave the school. The youth began to cry and pleaded, "Sir, please don't send me home. My father will be so disappointed; he's a minister and he has such high hopes for me.

Please sir, just give me one more chance. I will do my best to be a model student." Roberts thought for a few moments and said, "I tell you what, son. If you can find anybody who will invest a hundred dollars in your life in the next twenty-four hours, I will give you another chance."

The young man left the president's office hoping to find someone on campus to lend or give him a hundred dollars. But no one was willing to make the investment. The next day he walked into the building where the president's office was located. As he was sitting in the lobby waiting to see President Roberts, he held his tearful face in his hands. He heard someone walk by but did not pay attention to who it was. In a few moments he looked up and in the empty chair next to him was a sealed envelope with his name on it. He opened the envelope and there was a one-hundred dollar bill. He took the money to Oral Roberts and said, "President Roberts, I have a one-hundred dollar bill. Sir, you won't be sorry." That young man went on to be the class president and was graduated with honors. Only later did he learn that it was Oral Roberts who walked by and placed the envelope in the chair. The president who made the rules paid the price and made the investment in his life.

Walk Humbly

Finally, God expects us to walk humbly. We are called to have a daily, humble walk with God. Jesus said, "Blessed are the meek, For they shall inherit the earth" (Matthew 5:5).

Two friends, Albrecht and Franz, were struggling young artists. Since both were poor, they worked to support themselves while they studied. However, their daily work consumed too much of their time. Finally, they reached an agreement; they would draw lots, and one of them would work to support them while the other would study art at the university. Albrecht won and began to study, while Franz worked at hard labor to support them. They agreed that when Albrecht was successful he would support Franz who would then study art.

Albrecht Dürer went off to the universities of Europe to study. As the world knows, he not only had talent but also was an artistic genius. When he had attained success, he went back to keep his bargain with Franz. But Albrecht soon discovered the enormous price his friend had paid. For as Franz worked at hard labor to support his friend, his fingers had become stiff and twisted. His hands had been crippled with arthritis and ruined for life. He could no longer execute the delicate brush strokes necessary to paint. Though his artistic dreams could never be realized, he was not embittered but rejoiced in his friend's success.

One day Dürer came upon his friend unexpectedly. He found Franz kneeling with his gnarled hands intertwined in prayer. He was humbly praying for the success of his friend though he himself could no longer be an artist. Hurriedly Dürer sketched the folded hands of his humble friend. Today, this great masterpiece is known as "The Praying Hands."

What does God expect from me? God expects us to do what is right, to love mercy, and to walk humbly. Where will you be when you get where you're going . . . and you know what God expects from you?

Chapter 9

Are You Rock-Solid?

*When Jesus came into the region of Caesarea
Philippi, He asked His disciples, saying, "Who do
men say that I, the Son of Man, am?"
So they said, "Some say John the Baptist, some
Elijah, and others Jeremiah or one of the prophets."
He said to them, "But who do you say that I am?"
So Simon Peter answered and said, "You are the
Christ, the Son of the living God."
Jesus answered and said to him, "Blessed are you,
Simon Bar-Jonah, for flesh and blood has not revealed
this to you, but My Father who is in heaven. And I
say to you that you are Peter, and on this rock I will
build My church, and the gates of Hades shall not
prevail against it. And I will give you the keys of the
kingdom of heaven, and whatever you bind on earth
will be bound in heaven, and whatever you loose on
earth will be loosed in heaven."*

Then He commanded His disciples that they should
tell no one that He was Jesus the Christ
(Matthew 16:13-20).

. . . .

Sometimes it is easy to feel like the person who was riding in front on a bicycle built for two. When the pair came to a steep hill, it took a great deal of struggle for them to complete the climb. When they reached the top, the man peddling in front said to the other, "Man, that was a hard climb!" The guy in back said, "Yea, it sure was. And if I hadn't kept the brakes on all the way, we would have rolled down backwards."

Too often we put the brakes on the Christian faith. That is, we do not move forward from where we are to where we need to be. The result is that we become flimsy rather than solid in the Christian faith. How solid are we in the Christian faith? Are we really rock-solid for Jesus and His church? Do we move forward and yet feel that we are rolling backward in the faith?

Caesarea Philippi was located near the headwaters of the Jordan River. It was named for two rulers—Caesar Augustus and Philip the Tetrarch, son of Herod the Great. There was a house of worship built there in honor of the Greek god, Pan. This place in northern Galilee was vibrant with the rich symbolism of Rome and the philosophical influence of Greece.

It was somewhere in this area that Jesus must have stood, and as He looked into the distance, He turned to the twelve disciples and asked, "Who do men say that the Son of Man is?" The disciples generalized their responses, "Well, some say John the Baptizer. Others say you are Elijah, Jeremiah or one of the prophets."

Then Jesus turned the question directly to them. He was not trying to get a report of the latest rumor. He was not taking a public-opinion poll. He asked what *they* believed. He looked for their statement of faith: "But who do *you* say I am?"

It was Simon who blurted out that immortal answer, "You are the Christ, the Son of the living God." Jesus replied, "Blessed are you, Simon Bar-Jonah, for flesh and blood has not revealed this to you, but My Father who is in heaven. And I also say to you that you are Peter, and on this rock I will build My church, and the gates of Hades shall not prevail against it."

The Christian church was no accident. It did not just happen. It was not a sociological phenomenon, nor a quirk of history. The church was not founded upon a lie but upon the rock of God's truth. It was not a human invention. The church is a reality of hope for the salvation of the world.

The church is of God the Father, commissioned by Jesus, empowered and directed by the Holy Spirit. We are the church today because the Master continues to build His church. He has put the church here, and He has called us to be His church.

The explorers who first entered Peru found large, impressive buildings that may have stood for as long as two thousand years. These ancient Inca structures were built of hand-hewn rocks of different sizes and shapes. Some structures were three-sided, some four-sided and some seven-sided. The rocks were so perfectly cut and fitted together that they did not require the use of mortar. They stood for many centuries, even through earthquakes.

God continues to build His church in much the same way. One of the biblical images of the church is that of a building. It is not the building of a physical facility like a sanctuary or family life center, but the building made up of a community of believers. You and I, as believers, are the stones in the building. In his first letter, Peter says that we "as living stones, are being built up a spiritual house" (1 Peter 2:5). Paul tells us in Ephesians that we are "being fitted together . . . in the Lord, in whom you also are being built together for a dwelling place of God in the Spirit" (2:21-22).

The scriptural implication is that we are the living stones that God uses to build His church. After his great confession,

Jesus called Simon "Peter," which means "rock." Like Peter, God is calling us to be rock-solid. Let me ask you three rock-type questions.

Rock-Solid with the Message of the Church

First, are you rock-solid with the message of the church? A woman said to her pastor, "Pastor, I just don't know what to do. I grew up Methodist but became dissatisfied; I became a Baptist but that grew old; I've been a Presbyterian and an Episcopalian . . . I just do not know what to believe or what I am." The wise but blunt pastor replied, "Do not worry, my dear, it does not matter what label is on an empty bottle."

God's church is built upon the affirmation that Jesus Christ is God's only Son. Peter made the initial confession: "You are the Christ, the Son of the living God." This is the basic message of the church: Jesus Christ is the Savior of the world. He is Lord.

The world is full of religions, but there is only one true gospel. The world is full of religious teachers, but there is only one Savior. The great religions of the world teach salvation by human merit. Only the Christian faith teaches salvation by grace. All other religions say "do," but Christ says, "It is done! It is finished!"

Jesus did not bring a new religion—one that was a little better, more moral or more spiritual—to set alongside other religions. He came to set forth the gospel as the fulfillment for all human need. As the Son of God, He confronts us with God's offer to redeem humanity. He Himself is that offer. The gospel is Jesus Christ. He not only proclaimed the message but He is the message.

The message of the gospel is simply this: "For God so loved the world that He gave His only begotten Son, that whoever believes in Him should not perish but have everlasting life." The Christian faith is not merely a creed, a dogma or a set of rules. It is a personal relationship with the Risen Savior. Christ's work of salvation cannot be inherited and passed down, but must be individually received and experienced in our hearts by faith.

If Jesus is not the Christ, then we have nothing to offer the world. If Jesus is not the Christ, then we are no more than a civic club that meets on Sunday. The message of the church must be delivered in what we do; it must be embodied in who we are; and it must be proclaimed in what we believe. Are you rock-solid with the message?

Rock-Solid with the Mission of the Church

Second, are you rock-solid with the mission of the church? The mission is to spread the message of the Master. Jesus entrusted the disciples and His followers with this mission.

This does not mean we simply announce that Jesus is the Christ and go home. It does not mean we just sit in our beautiful new sanctuaries with smiles on our faces while the world quickly self-destructs.

Two American jet fighters were flying in formation. They had just started their descent when the lead pilot radioed, "I've lost my wing man." One of the two planes had gone down. Immediately, workers in the control tower picked up the "red" phone that was connected to the rescue-helicopter team on stand-by duty. When the red phone is picked up, a rescue team is to respond immediately and be in the air within two minutes.

The lead pilot descended below the clouds looking for his wing man. He saw that he had bailed out and was in the ocean. The pilot circled helplessly overhead while his friend struggled in the water. "My wing man is tangled in his parachute. Have you notified the helicopter?" he said desperately. "He's floating, but having a difficult time getting his life raft inflated. Have you commissioned the helicopter?" Minutes later the control tower heard another message, "It's still not inflated. He's beginning to sink. Where's the rescue team?" Minutes later another plea came, "He's above water, but still struggling. Where's the helicopter?" Seconds later the pilot said, "He's now underwater. Where's the helicopter?" In desperation the pilot yelled, "I can't see him now. I fear we've lost him. Where's the helicopter?"

Where was the helicopter? It never got to the scene. Later, an investigation revealed that the rescue team had decided to do some shopping at a PX some fifty miles away from base. They were so busy taking care of themselves, they never heard the cries for help.

The multitudes are all around us. Many are plunging toward their own demise. Some are already in the water without a life raft. Some are still floating, treading water and growing weary. Others are beginning to sink as the parachute lines of complex living entangle them. Who is the rescue team? Where are they now? Do they hear the calls for help?

The church is God's rescue team. Multitudes of people need to be rescued. Families are coming apart. Teenagers are losing themselves in drugs, sex and suicide. Social and moral issues threaten to tear the very fabric that holds our society together. Are you rock-solid and ready to "go and make disciples of all nations"?

Rock-Solid with the Master of the Church

Third, are you rock-solid with the Master of the church? Who is Jesus to you? We know what the world says, "He was a great teacher and interpreter of Jewish Scriptures." Others say, "He was a great philosopher on the order of Socrates or Plato." Still others declare, "He was a great prophet." Say some, "On a par with Mohammed or Buddha."

Then there are those who state, "He is obsolete, an anachronism from a bygone age with little relevance for the twenty-first century." Josh McDowell is right on target when he writes, "Either Christ was a lunatic, a liar, or the living Lord."

We know what the world says. More important is what the Scripture says. Isaiah writes, "For unto us a Child is born, Unto us a Son is given; And the government will be upon His shoulder; And His name will be called Wonderful, Counselor, Mighty God, Everlasting Father, Prince of Peace."

Malachi calls him the "Son of Righteousness . . . with healing in His wings."

Paul in his letter to Timothy calls him the, "One Mediator between God and men." Peter in his epistle calls him "the Chief Shepherd." John in his letter from the Isle of Patmos calls him, "The Alpha and the Omega" and "KING OF KINGS AND LORD OF LORDS."

Who do you say He is? Many of us would say, "He is the Savior of the world!" But is Christ *your* Savior?

I had heard the Good News many times. Yet there came a time when I not only heard but I believed. I did trust in Christ, Christ alone, for the forgiveness of my sins and the salvation of my life. There was another realization also. Not only did I believe in Christ, I knew that He believed in me.

Have you seen the movie, *Mr. Holland's Opus*? It is a wonderful story of a dedicated music teacher named Glen Holland. At the beginning of his career, Mr. Holland dreams of becoming a famous composer. He dreams of living in Hollywood, making lots of money, and writing theme songs for movies. But he never fulfills his dream.

After getting married, he realizes that he has to feed his family and pay the mortgage. So he takes a job at the local high school as a music teacher. He spends his entire career working with students at the John F. Kennedy High School. With great tenderness, he works with a redheaded girl with pigtails. She wanted so much to play the clarinet, but had a terrible time finding the right notes. No one believed in her or took time to help her, except Mr. Holland. With great compassion, he worked with an African-American student who wanted to learn to play the drums, but he had a difficult time finding the beat. With great patience, he worked with a street-wise, tough kid named Lenny. Lenny had a lousy attitude and was mad at the world, but Mr. Holland's positive attitude began to pay dividends. Mr. Holland helped them all and hundreds more like them.

At the conclusion of the movie, the school loses the funding for its music program and Mr. Holland retires. As he cleans out his room, he tells his devoted wife and his deaf son that he feels like a failure. He never accomplished his great dream. He never went to Hollywood. He never became a famous composer. With slumped shoulders, he heads out of the school. Then he hears a noise in the auditorium and the teacher in him has to investigate. He opens the door and is surprised to see that the auditorium is packed with his former students. As he walks in they give him a long thunderous standing ovation while chanting his name. They had come back to express their love and appreciation to this man who had given his life to them.

The little girl with the red pigtails, who had grown up and was now the governor of the state, approached the microphone. She said, "Mr. Holland, we know that you never got to become the famous composer you dreamed of being. But don't you see it today? Your greatest composition is what you did with us, your students. Mr. Holland, look around you. We are your great opus! We are the music of your life."

In one sense, we are the Master's great opus. We are His great composition, and He desires to make His heavenly music through you and me on this earth. The Master is building His church, and we are to be the rock-solid pieces of His church. We are called to exalt and glorify His name, and to proclaim His words of life.

Where will you be when you get where you're going . . . by becoming rock-solid with the message and the mission of the Master of the church?

Chapter 10

Keepers of the Flame

*The Lord spoke to Moses, saying, "Command Aaron
and his sons, saying, 'This is the law of burnt offering:
The burnt offering shall be on the hearth upon the altar
all night until morning, and the fire of the altar shall be
kept burning on it. And the priest shall put on his linen
garment, and his linen trousers he shall put on his body,
and take up the ashes of the burnt offering which the
fire has consumed on the altar, and he shall put them
beside the altar. Then he shall take off his garments,
put on other garments, and carry the ashes outside the
camp to a clean place. And the fire on the altar shall be
kept burning on it; it shall not be put out. And the
priest shall burn wood on it every morning, and lay the
burnt offering in order on it; and he shall burn on it the
fat of the peace offerings. A fire shall always be burning
on the altar; it shall never go out.'" (Leviticus 6:8-13).*

More than any other book in the Old Testament, the book of Leviticus challenges God's people to live a holy life. It is not sufficient that God's people merely have a place for public worship. What we do in church determines in part who we will be out in the world. In one sense, all the sacrifices and commitments we make go for naught if they do not produce holy living.

This passage in the sixth chapter describes how the Levitical priests were to handle burnt offerings. The Levites had many duties, but one among them stood supreme. Other duties could be postponed. Other tasks could be deferred. But there was one duty they had to tend to with daily care. It was simply this: The fire on the altar was to be kept burning. This fire was the visible symbol of God's presence among the people. It was a sacred fire and it was not to be extinguished.

Of course, we are far removed from those ancient days and customs. We no longer worship with incense and burnt offerings. We no longer maintain an altar with a burning flame on which sacrifices are offered to God. However, in a spiritual sense, we are challenged to keep the fire of the Holy Spirit burning on the altar of our hearts.

In 1784 in Baltimore Francis Asbury was consecrated the first Methodist bishop. He traveled over 250,000 miles on horseback and literally rode three horses to death (their names were Jane, Spark and Fox). Asbury preached over 16,500 sermons and witnessed thousands of conversions. Toward the end of his life, he made the following entry into his *Journal:* "My body is weak!" This was certainly an understatement. Asbury suffered from asthma, boils, bronchitis, fever, neuralgia and tuberculosis, which finally ended his earthly life. Asbury wrote, "Yet, I gladly bear all of these things for the sake of the elect. . . . But this does not concern me like the want of more grace. My heart is too cool toward God. I want to feel Him like a holy flame." Now there is a real Methodist!

The point is this: For Christians there should be an inner flame of devotion for God. Burning on the altar of our hearts should be the consecration of our lives to God. If we are to reflect the light of Christ in the world, then this inner fire of devotion must burn brightly. Whatever else Christians choose to do or not do, the sacred fire of God's Spirit on the altar of our hearts must be nurtured daily and kept burning. It must never go out!

A craftsman became famous for his stained-glass windows. He once told about a time when a young apprentice came to him and asked if he could borrow his tools. The craftsman asked him, "But why do you want to borrow them?" The young apprentice said, "I'm very dissatisfied with my work. I'd like to use your tools to see if I can do better work."

A week later the craftsman went to the young apprentice and said, "Well, how are things going?" The young man replied, "Not so good, sir." One of the older artists in the workshop overheard the conversation and interrupted the young man to say, "You not only need the tools of your master, you need his fire!"

John Wesley was once asked why so many people came to hear him preach. He replied, "God set me on fire, and people come to watch me burn." Wesley was empowered by God's Spirit. The altar of his heart was burning with devotion to His Lord!

Unfortunately, in a world like ours today are many threats to the spiritual life. If we leave these unchecked, they can easily extinguish the inner fires of our devotion to God. Here are three dangers.

The Danger of Exhaustion

First, exhaustion is a danger to the fire burning in our hearts. A fire cannot burn without fuel. Flames go out due to a lack of fuel. The Levitical priests had to ensure a ready supply of wood. Whenever the flame on the altar burned down, they brought more fuel to the altar fires.

Physical exhaustion or mental fatigue can dampen the flame burning in our hearts. It is so important to retreat periodically and refuel. Did you realize that during Jesus' three years of active ministry, he made ten periods of retreat? This was in addition to the nightly rest and the Sabbath rest.

Someone once said, "There is no music in a rest, but there is the making of music in it." God writes the music of our lives. It is up to us whether or not we will be in harmony with Him. In the melody of our lives, the music may be broken here and there by periods of "rests." We may think we have come to the end of the song. (This is especially true if you are a workaholic.) There may be times of forced rest through sickness, disappointment or frustrated efforts.

Moses was at Rephidim while Joshua led the Israelites in battle. As long as the soldiers could see Moses with his arms stretched up in the air, the battle went in favor of the Israelites. But Moses' arms grew weary. It does not take a biblical scholar to figure out that Moses was at a point of physical exhaustion. When Moses dropped his arms, the battle went against the Israelites. Aaron and Hur came to his side and held his arms up. Consequently, the Israelites went on to victory. We must have periods of rest and retreat to ensure victory in the Christian life.

The Danger of Neglect

Second, neglect is a danger to the fire burning in our hearts. For the priests in ancient Israel, neglect was a constant threat. There was nothing terribly exciting about watching a fire burn for hours in the temple, especially during the night. Going through the motions day after day made for a perfunctory religious observance, especially for the priests.

When people fall away from the faith, it does not necessarily happen overnight. They do not get up one day and say, "Well, I'm not going to have any more to do with God, the Bible or the church." It does not happen instantaneously. It usually happens gradually and by neglect. If the spiritual life is neglected, then the inner flame becomes smaller until it becomes a flicker, thereby in danger of dying out.

Living things die through neglect. A house plant, a garden, a friendship or a marriage will gradually wither when not nourished. Most people give greater attention to beginning a relationship than they do to cultivating a relationship.

The same is true with the Christian faith. What the church has called "the means of grace" is laid aside slowly in favor of other things. Actually, neglect is, unhappily, too common in the Christian life. Parts of the Bible are difficult to read and understand. At times prayers seem repetitious and offered to an unresponsive ear. Weekly worship too easily becomes predictable and routine.

What is the remedy for neglect? First, we must become aware of the neglect and make a conscious effort to do something about it. Second, we must discipline ourselves daily.

Discipline is having borders in our lives. It is not meant to restrict but to expand. Discipline is essential in the Christian life. Without discipline, there can be no sustained growth. We may have determination but if we lack discipline to carry it out, it is useless. A successful prayer life needs discipline. Daily devotions need sustenance. Weekly worship needs vitality. Christian fellowship needs intentionality.

Recently *National Geographic* featured an article about the Alaskan bull moose. In the fall breeding season, the male population of this rugged animal does battle constantly. They literally go head to head with antlers crunching together as they collide. If the antlers are broken, this brings defeat for that moose. The heftiest moose, the one with the largest and strongest antlers, usually triumphs. Therefore, the battle fought in the fall is actually won during the summer months when the moose feeds on a diet that grows antlers.

Here is a lesson for us. Spiritual battles await all of us. Satan will choose a season to attack. Will we be victorious or will we fall? Much depends on what we digest now into our daily devotional life. Neglect in the spiritual life is a danger to the fire burning in our hearts.

The Danger of Compromise

Finally, compromise is a danger to the fire burning in our hearts. There is a profound difference between a healthful flexibility and unwholesome compromise. When deeply held convictions are bartered away, the flame of inner devotion to God is compromised. When moral values are sullied in trade-offs for power, recognition or security, more is lost than gained.

Jesus asked, "What will [you] gain by winning the whole world, at the cost of losing [your] soul?" (Luke 9:25, NEB)

The issue of compromise touches what we think we are when we stand before the mirror of conscience, and what we really are when we stand in the presence of God. Compromise quenches the flame, dimming both the vision and the desire for God. Moral character and spiritual conviction rekindle our devotion and dedication.

Years ago a primitive tribe was discovered deep in the jungles of South America. Anthropologists learned that the most important role within the tribe was the keeper of the flame. Since fire was so precious—and took such effort to recreate—one member was entrusted with the responsibility of keeping the flame alive. His responsibility was to keep the fire alive, even when the tribe moved to another location. His was a vital task.

That role is important not only in every tribe and culture, but especially in the church. God is calling us to be the keepers of the flame of His holy Word. God is calling us to be the keepers of the flame of His redeeming love. God is calling us to be the keepers of the flame of His righteousness and truth.

If the flame is not kept alive, values die, morals are distorted and people suffer. Will you be a keeper of the flame?

Christians have an altar on the heart where fire burns for the Lord. The flame there requires continuous rekindling by the Holy Spirit. On this altar rests the deep allegiance of a life given to God. Keep the fire burning. Don't ever, ever let that flame go out.

Where will you be when you get where you're going . . . by keeping the flame burning?

Chapter 11

Don't Panic!

You, Israel, are My servant, Jacob whom I have chosen, The descendents of Abraham My friend. You whom I have taken from the ends of the earth, And called from its farthest regions, And said to you, "You are My servant, I have chosen you and have not cast you away: Fear not, for I am with you; Be not dismayed, for I am your God. I will strengthen you, Yes, I will help you, I will uphold you with My righteous right hand. Behold, all those who were incensed against you Shall be ashamed and disgraced; They shall be as nothing, And those who strive with you shall perish. You shall seek them and not find them—Those who contended with you. Those who war against you Shall be as nothing, As a nonexistent thing. For I, the Lord your God, will hold your right hand, Saying to you, 'Fear not, I will help you'" (Isaiah 41:8-13).

. . . .

It happened on October 23, 1982. Four people in the bleachers of a football field in Monterey Park, California, suddenly became nauseous and dizzy. Feeling a common illness, they left the bleachers and talked to the officials. An investigation discovered that they all had a soft drink from a vendor at the refreshment stand. The officials did not want to take a chance. They announced to the entire crowd watching the football game that if anyone had this particular soft drink they might become ill. They then rushed these four persons to the emergency room. By the time the ambulance got back to the football stadium, 150 people were now suffering from nausea—and filled with panic. The following twenty-four hours revealed that nothing was wrong with the syrup or the water. Something else had caused the dizziness in the four people. But panic had caused the illness in all the rest.

Panic is known to all of us. It is now reaching epidemic proportions in our society. The word "panic" literally means "a sudden, overpowering, often contagious terror."

How about this ambiguous message on an elevator: "In case of an emergency, don't panic. Simply press the red button"? But printed on top of the red button were these words, "Panic Button."

We wait for the doctor's analysis and prognosis; we feel dread and agitation. Or perhaps long-expected news comes in a letter about something that we had planned for, hoped for or longed for. Should we open it? Our hands quiver. We wonder. Panic attacks us!

The boss calls us into his office. He says, "We are going to lay you off." Panic hits us.

We enter a room and are shunned by a friend. Panic grips us.

A spouse grows cold in a marital relationship. Panic attacks us. Children do not turn out the way parents had hoped. Panic surrounds us.

A student walks into class to take an exam but discovers that he is unprepared. Panic finds us.

We have all felt panic at one time or another. Robert Burns was right on target when he wrote, "If each man's internal care were written upon his brow, / Those who have our envy would have our pity now."

I have often discovered that panic grips some of the great leaders and heroes of the faith, people who are mature Christians, who live with greater strength and courage than I ever thought possible for my life.

Some of us may say, "But how can Christians panic?" So we try to push it down and hide our foreboding. Although it may be out of sight, it is still in mind. The agitation rages within.

God has given us a prescription for panic in Isaiah 41. He has told us what to do when panic strikes. When news comes that agitates us, when the loss or potential loss of something or someone we love is communicated to us, when we are worried or fearful, God tells us not to panic.

He speaks to all the nations. He then turns and speaks tenderly to His nation, Israel. After reaffirming His love for them, He says, "Fear not, for I am with you; Be not dismayed, for I am your God. I will strengthen you, Yes, I will help you, I will uphold you with My righteous right hand."

The Hebrew word translated "dismayed" is not accurate. It literally means "to look around with anxious panic." When distress overtakes us or bad news hits us, we often look around and say, "What in the world am I going to do? Whom should I call? What should I say? How can I face this situation?" Here is a helpful method of responding to crisis.

Reaffirm the Presence of the Lord

First, reaffirm the presence of the Lord. Through Isaiah, God says, "Do not fear, for I am with you. Be not dismayed, for I am your God." This means that we must unlearn a long-held heresy, that God is with us only when things are working well. We tend to think that when the course of life is smooth, God is present, kind, gracious and benevolent. But if life is rocky doubt begins to build: Is God truly with us? So we come out on the other end of our thinking with the conclusion, "God must have withdrawn His presence from me." Because we don't pause in life's tragedies and disappointments to sense God's presence, we ask the age-old question, "Where are you, God?"

Whatever your situation or circumstance, God is present. Remember when Jesus had His disciples cross the Sea of Galilee by boat while He went to the mountain to pray alone. A storm quickly came up on the sea and the boat was in grave danger. But between three and six o'clock in the morning Jesus came to them, walking on the sea. In the darkness, the disciples were stricken with panic and they cried, "It's a ghost." "But Jesus immediately spoke to them, saying, 'Be of good cheer! It is I; do not be afraid'" (Matthew 14:27).

Three passengers were flying together on a chartered twin-engine airplane. One was a Boy Scout, another a nuclear scientist and the third a Roman Catholic priest. They introduced themselves to each other and spoke of their purpose for getting away over the weekend. The Boy Scout was going to camp out in the wilderness and earn merit badges toward his Eagle Scout award. The priest was getting away to pray and meditate for the weekend. The nuclear scientist, however, was so arrogant about his intellect, he monopolized the whole conversation. He made it known to the Boy Scout and priest just how smart he really was. In fact, he told them that he was the smartest man in the world. He was getting away to solve some of the major problems of society.

Suddenly, the plane developed engine trouble. As they flew over the mountains losing altitude, it became obvious that the plane was going down. The young pilot panicked and bailed out, but just before he jumped he yelled to his three passengers, "Only two parachutes are left, and you three will have to decide who will use them."

As the pilot jumped, the nuclear scientist looked at the Boy Scout and priest and said, "Well, there is no real problem here. I am the smartest man in the world. I have to be saved. The world needs my brain." So the nuclear scientist jumped out of the plane. The priest fell to his knees and began to pray. The Boy Scout tapped him on the shoulder and said, "Mister, your prayers have been answered." He looked at the Boy Scout and said, "Son, how can that be? There is only one parachute left. I've lived a long and productive life and I'm committed to the Lord. You take it and save yourself." The Boy Scout said, "No sweat! We're both going to be saved!" The priest replied, "But how can that be?" The Boy Scout responded, "The smartest man in the world just jumped out with my knapsack on his back!"

God is with us in all the circumstances of life. He has promised never to leave nor forsake us. There may be times when we feel that the situation is hopeless, and we want to bail out of life. We need to remember that our Lord is present to redeem the situation at hand for His glory and our good.

Resist the Panic

Second, resist the panic. God said, "I will strengthen you. I will help you." Don't call on undependable resources for hope or relief. Don't call on other gods. God told Isaiah to say, "Tell them that I am their God. Don't cast about looking for other solutions. Don't be dismayed by any news that comes to you, for I am with you and I am your God."

When you are in a panic situation, step back and remember how God worked in other situations. I have known God personally for more than twenty years. Each year has brought traumatic experiences in which I have built up a reservoir of memories of the reliability of God. Regardless of whatever might happen, I can remember how God worked in other situations and so I trust Him with the situation at hand.

It is interesting to note that in English translations of Isaiah 41:10, the last three verbs are in the future tense. "I will strengthen you . . . I will help you . . . I will uphold you with My righteous right hand." But in the Hebrew they are in the present perfect tense: "I have strengthened you. I have helped you. I have upheld you with my righteous right hand."

Gather your sacred memories of how God came to you in lonely watches of the night. Remember how He intervened in situations that you could not possibly have worked out. As you recall those times of crisis and the way God worked, these become your resources for dealing with panic. You can rest in the assurance that He is working in that situation or with that person in the present Now!

God Will Resolve Your Problems

Third, recognize the ultimate resolution of the problem that is causing the panic. God reviewed for Israel the eventual destruction of their enemies. He says, "Listen, what is causing your panic cannot ultimately defeat you. You belong to me. Death is not the end. Sickness cannot destroy you. What people say or do to you cannot hurt you. You're mine." Suddenly, in the midst of the panic quietness comes to rest upon us and to still our fearful hearts.

Finally, we need to put our hand into His hand. "I will uphold you with my righteous right hand." The right hand of God is not only the presence of Christ with us; it is the very authority of God Himself.

In prayer we meet God face to face! Whatever needs you have, place them in your right hand. Then give your right hand to God, knowing that the righteous right hand of God will take hold of your hand. We serve a God who takes us by the hand and says, "Don't panic!"

Where will you be when you get where you're going, even when panic grips your life?

Chapter 12

Kyrios! Kyrios!

"Not everyone who says to Me, 'Lord, Lord,' shall enter the kingdom of heaven, but he who does the will of My Father in heaven. Many will say to Me in that day, 'Lord, Lord, have we not prophesied in Your name, cast out demons in Your name, and done many wonders in Your name?' And then I will declare to them, 'I never knew you; depart from Me, you who practice lawlessness!'" (Matthew 7:21-23).

The Sermon on the Mount is the greatest sermon of all time. Jesus gave this sermon on the northern side of the Sea of Galilee. The scene was a crowd of curious, uncommitted followers pressing in around a smaller group of committed disciples. These serious disciples were devoted to Jesus not only as an authoritative Teacher but also as the living Lord.

In the Greek New Testament the word for "Lord" is "*Kyrios*." This word is found over seven hundred times throughout Scripture. What does "*kyrios*" literally mean? A capsule definition would be "one who is ruler and authority over a domain." If we apply that definition to the Christian life, we are saying that "Jesus Christ is the ruler and authority over the domain of my life." Do we really mean this when we make the affirmation, "Jesus is Lord"?

We have been trained in God-talk. We say the right things. We recite the affirmations of faith in worship services. We memorize Bible verses in Sunday school classes. But does our lifestyle reflect what we say? Does our "doing" reflect our "being" under the lordship of Christ?

It is possible to be a follower of Jesus Christ without being His disciple. Someone was once talking to a great scholar about a young man. He said, "I understand he was one of your students." The teacher answered sternly, "He may have attended one of my lectures, but he was not one of my students." There is a world of difference between attending lectures and being a student.

It is one of the handicaps that exist in the church today. Many are distant followers of Jesus Christ but not enough are disciples! A disciple is not only a follower but also one who is under the authority of Jesus' lordship.

The game of baseball can illustrate the point. First base represents the lordship of Christ. Second base represents our church membership and the activities we do in the name of Christ. Third base represents the good works we do in the community. Home plate represents heaven. The ball of life is pitched to each one of us. We stand at the plate and we take a swing at life. We hit the ball way out into center field. We get excited about all the possibilities that the world is presenting to us. So we start running around the bases so fast that we miss tagging first base. We then run to second base and purposely step onto the bag with our church membership and activities. We make it to third base and even have time to catch our breath because we have accomplished many good works in the community. Then, one day we come sliding into homeplate. We think we have hit a home run. But when the dust of life has cleared away, the Great Umpire of the universe will say, "You're out!" We might argue with the Umpire and present our case, "But I beat the ball by a mile!" But the Umpire will reply, "You're out because you missed first base." Is Jesus Christ the Lord of your life? Does your life exhibit the lordship of Christ?

Let's write out the word "LORD" in an acrostic form. Each letter will stand for something: L – O – R – D.

Loyalty to Christ

The first letter is "L." This letter represents *loyalty* to Christ. Where is the allegiance of your heart? Is it to Christ and His church? What are your priorities?

A story about John Gray and his friend, Bob, is a story of loyalty. They were inseparable friends. From the day they first met, they ate from the same table, lived in the same house. They were simply friends, but they were the best of friends. In public they were never apart. They took walks together every day. At home they greeted and entertained guests together. The day came that John Gray died. He was buried in an English cemetery. Throughout his illness Bob never left John Gray's side. Now Bob watched his friend's body being lowered into its resting place. When the graveside service was over, everyone left the cemetery but Bob. He was still there at dusk mourning the loss of his best friend.

Finally, he was persuaded by friends to go home, but he was back at the cemetery the next morning. In fact Bob went back to the graveside of John Gray nearly every day for several years. Then one day he was found lifeless by the graveside.

John Gray would probably not be remembered today if it had not been for Bob's loyalty. There is a water fountain in Edinburgh today as a memorial to that loyalty. By the way, Bob was a little wiry-haired Scottish terrier! If a dog can be that loyal to a man, how much more should we be loyal to Jesus Christ?

Jesus said, "No servant can serve two masters; for either he will hate the one and love the other, or else he will hold to the one and despise the other. You cannot serve God and mammon" (Luke 16:13).

Obedience to Christ

The letter "O" represents *obedience* to Christ. We often know what Christ wants us to do but we find it difficult to carry out in obedience. This is a matter of the will.

What is the desire of your heart? Is it to truly be obedient to Jesus Christ? Are you obedient in your Christian life? In your devotional life? In your church attendance? In your service to the church? In your tithes and offerings? In your witnessing for Christ to others?

Little Johnny's mother asked him to stand up and greet guests who were approaching the house. His little five-year-old mind was stubborn and he refused to do so. His mom gave him several warnings, and he finally decided to stand up. As he walked to the front door with his mother, he reluctantly said: "Mom, I may be standing up on the outside, but I'm still sitting down on the inside."

A lot of us may be like this in our obedience to Christ. We obey because we know that is what our minister, spouse, parents or another expects of us. We may stand up for Jesus on the outside but we're still sitting down on the inside. Jesus said: "If you love me, you will keep my commandments" (John 14:15, RSV). Love for the Master is the proper motivation for obedience. Obedience flows out of a grateful and loving heart. To be obedient to Christ because we love Him comes as His Word richly dwells in us.

Training the king's horses in Arabia is a tedious task. The primary lesson is obedience. For example, whenever the trainer blows his whistle a certain way, the horses must learn to run toward him. The training goes on for months, and then an interesting test is given. For several days the horses are deprived of water, until they become frantic with thirst and pace excitedly around the fenced-in area. Then suddenly the gate leading to the oasis is opened, and the horses rush toward the water to quench their thirst. But just as they are about to drink, the trainer blows his whistle. The horses instinctively stop where they are. A tremendous struggle goes on within them. There is the desire to stoop and drink, but their wills have been trained to obey the command of the master. Those horses that turn away from the water at this critical moment and run back to the trainer are the only ones considered fit for the service of the king.

In like manner, those children of God who have learned to be sensitive to the leading of the Spirit and to obey the will of the Father at all times are the only ones fit for the service of the King of kings.

Reaching for Christ

The letter "R" means *reaching* out for Christ. If you write the word "preacher" and erase the "p," you have the word "reacher." Now you may not be called to be a preacher but if you are a Christian and you say, "Jesus is Lord," then you will be a reacher for Christ. You reach out to others not only with your talk but also with your daily life. Living under the lordship of Christ is practical and applicable in everyday situations.

Over one hundred years ago, a great fire broke out in Chicago. Eyewitness accounts report that it was like hell on earth. For those who were trapped, the only place of safety was running to Lake Michigan. Thousands of people went into the lake that night and waded out as far as they could go. One little girl was found near the edge of the shore crying.

A preacher in the crowd noticed her. He tried to comfort her in the midst of the panic. "I know you are separated from your parents, but we'll find them." But she kept crying. He said, "Honey, you're safe." She said, "I know I'm safe, but I'm crying because I did not bring anybody with me." We are under a biblical mandate to bring others with us into the kingdom of God.

Determination

The last letter "D" stands for *determination.* Are you determined to be loyal, to be obedient, and to reach out? We cannot remain determined if we are uncertain of who Jesus is and of our salvation. The wisdom of humanity is foolishness to God. Paul seemed to say, "Until we see Christ, we will all look through a glass dimly" (1 Corinthians 13:12).

Many Christians today are simply not determined. Jesus said, "No one, having put his hand to the plow, and looking back, is fit for the kingdom of God" (Luke 9:62). Are you determined to let Jesus be Lord of all regardless of what it may cost you?

A story in chapter five of Luke tells of four men who took their paralyzed friend to see Jesus. They were determined to see Jesus. When they couldn't get him inside the house where Jesus was ministering because of crowds, they climbed up on the roof and tore a hole in the roof. They then lowered the paralyzed man into Jesus' presence where he could receive his healing.

That is determination, the kind of determination that we need each day, the kind to help us experience Jesus Christ as Lord. Different kinds of paralysis invade our lives: pride, unforgiveness, greed, anger and self-righteousness. The good news is that Jesus can heal paralysis of any sort.

A vaccine that missionaries must take when they travel to certain countries protects them against jungle diseases. When one gets the shot, the next day he feels flu-like symptoms. But what one has is a little bit of certain jungle diseases, just enough to keep from getting the real thing should one be exposed to it.

Some people have just enough religion to keep them from getting the real thing, a living and vital relationship with Jesus Christ. They have just enough of the formalities and rituals to keep from experiencing the real thing. They may possess the form of religion but they do not know the substantive power of Jesus Christ.

This is the crisis of the church in America today: "having a form of godliness but denying its power" (2 Timothy 3:5). John Wesley feared that something like this would happen to the great Methodist movement. In 1786, he wrote, "I am not afraid that the people called Methodists should ever cease to exist either in Europe or America. But I am afraid, lest they should only exist as a dead sect, having the form of religion without power."

Where will you be when you get where you're going . . . by living under the lordship of Jesus Christ?

Biographical Sketch of Dr. Lenny Stadler

D r. Leonard E. Stadler is an ordained Elder and has served for 21 years in the Western North Carolina Annual Conference of the United Methodist Church. He holds the Bachelor of Arts degree in Religion from Elon College, the Master of Divinity degree from Duke Divinity School, and the Doctor of Ministry degree in Spiritual Formation from Asbury Theological Seminary.

Dr. Stadler was the 1995 clergy recipient of the Denman Evangelism Award in the Western North Carolina Annual Conference. He has held over 125 revivals and camp meetings throughout the Southeastern Jurisdiction of the United Methodist Church.

Prior to his Christian conversion, "Lenny" played bass for a nationally known music group called "Blackfoot." But his ambition left him spiritually empty, restless and hopeless. His compelling story of God's transforming grace from rock musician to United Methodist minister is stirring and challenging.

Powerful and straightforward, the preaching ministry of Dr. Stadler challenges Christians today to press beyond superficial religion to recover the New Testament fervor and joy of a personal relationship with Jesus Christ. With his wife, Shana (formerly of Dallas and a United Methodist minister's daughter), and their children, Shalen and LenPaul, he serves Weddington United Methodist Church in Weddington, North Carolina.

Under Dr. Stadler's preaching ministry and pastoral leadership, since 1989 Weddington United Methodist Church has become one of the fastest growing United Methodist churches in the Southeast. In the past ten years, the church has received over 2000 full members and now averages a weekly worship attendance exceeding 1200. The Weddington church recently completed a new three million dollar sanctuary and additional education space to accommodate the growth.